# Decoding the RSS

Raosaheb Kasbe

# Decoding the RSS
## Its Tradition and Politics

Translated from the Marathi by
**Deepak Borgave**

Edited by
**Vinutha Mallya**

With an Introduction by
**Shamsul Islam**

Offset edition first published in July 2019.
Reprinted December 2019.
Digital print edition, January 2020.

LeftWord Books
2254/2A Shadi Khampur
New Ranjit Nagar
New Delhi 110008
INDIA

LeftWord Books is the publishing division of
Naya Rasta Publishers Pvt. Ltd.

First published in Marathi as *Zot*
by Janbodh Prakashan, Pune, 1978

leftword.com

ISBN 978-81-940778-2-4

In memory of

COMRADE GOVIND PANSARE,

DR. NARENDRA DABHOLKAR,

DR. M.M. KALBURGI,

and

GAURI LANKESH,

who laid their lives

fighting against

fundamentalism

# CONTENTS

# DREAMING A HINDU RASHTRA

SHAMSUL ISLAM

*Decoding the RSS* is the English translation of Raosaheb Kasbe's well-known Marathi book *Zot* ('Searchlight') on the Rashtriya Swayamsevak Sangh (RSS). Raosaheb Kasbe is a renowned political scientist, a leading scholar of Dalit movements and Hindutva politics in India. Over the decades, he has watched closely the RSS spreading its tentacles in Maharashtra, as well as the rest of India. *Zot* is an incisive study of the most important ideological treatise of the RSS, *Bunch of Thoughts* (1966, titled *Vichardhan* in Marathi), a collection of the writings, speeches and interviews of Madhav Sadashiv Golwalkar. Golwalkar is the preeminent ideologue of the RSS, and was its second, and longest-serving, *sarsanghchalak* (supreme leader), from 1940 to 1973. The book, the bible for RSS cadres, presents the ideological case for converting the democratic-secular Indian polity into a Hindu *rashtra*, where the *Manusmruti* would be law and the *varna* system would be strictly adhered to. To explain the RSS's worldview, Kasbe quotes extensively from this book, so that no misrepresentation could be claimed. The RSS does not stand for an egalitarian India but a *Hindu-sthan* (Hindu nation) under Brahminical hegemony, harking back to the times of the Peshwas.

Professor Kasbe's concern about RSS, the most prominent

flag-bearer of Hindutva politics, was natural, as it came into being in opposition to the resurgence of Dalit politics in Maharashtra. It may be interesting to note that Hindutva politics originated mainly in areas—now part of Maharashtra—where Brahminism was challenged in a sustained manner by Shudra icons like Tukaram, Namdev, Shahuji Maharaj, Jotiba Phule, Savitribai Phule and Dr. B.R. Ambedkar.

*Zot* appeared in 1978 when the RSS was trying to capture the Janata Party, which had won the election after the Emergency was lifted in 1977. *Zot* became an instant hit with political activists. It exposes the doublespeak of the RSS and the potent threat it poses to Indian democracy. This irrefutable exposure created immediate ripples, especially among RSS zealots who, instead of countering Kasbe's arguments, chose the fascist method of burning copies of the book at Pune while the Janata Party's session was on. Clearly, *Zot* had hit a raw nerve.

Kasbe shows how the RSS countered the united freedom struggle by declaring that Hindus and Muslims, and followers of all other religions, constituted separate nations, and became the most vocal votary of the two-nation theory. It further asserted that since India was primordially a Hindu nation, all other 'nations', especially Muslims, must accept the hegemony of Hindus. For the RSS, the main enemy was not the colonial masters, but the united freedom struggle itself, since it militated against the idea of the Hindu *rashtra*.

HINDU RASHTRA VERSUS
COMPOSITE INDIAN NATIONALISM

It is not a coincidence that the RSS was born when the united freedom struggle was trying to overcome the communal divide. Those who were killed at Jallianwala Bagh in Amritsar on April 13, 1919, included 220 Hindus, 94 Sikhs and 61 Muslims. Of the 19 peasants hanged after the Chauri Chaura incident on February 5, 1922, in the Gorakhpur district of the United Provinces, six were Muslims. Another milestone in the Indian freedom struggle, the robbery of the British government's treasury at Kakori on August 9, 1925, was conceived by Ram Prasad Bismil and Ashfaqullah Khan. They were hanged on the same day—December 19, 1927.

The RSS was founded in 1925 by Keshav Baliram Hedgewar (1889–1940), who remained its *sarsanghchalak* till his death. Hedgewar was initially a Congressman. His reason for leaving the Congress in the early 1920s has been described in an RSS publication as follows:

> It is clear that Gandhiji worked constantly with one eye on Hindu–Muslim unity. . . . But Doctorji [Hedgewar] sensed danger in that move. In fact, he did not even relish the newfangled slogan of 'Hindu–Muslim unity'.[1]

Hedgewar thirsted for communal conflict. His biography tells us that when sometimes *bandwallahs* hesitated to play music in front of mosques, Hedgewar 'himself would take over the drums and rouse the dormant manliness of the Hindus'.[2]

The RSS, under both Hedgewar and Golwalkar, not only took no part in the freedom struggle, but actively discouraged those who wanted to. Golwalkar writes,

> There is another reason for the need of always remaining involved in routine work. There is some unrest in the mind due to the situation developing in the country from time to time. There was such unrest in 1942. Before that there was the movement in 1930–31. At that time many other people had gone to Doctorji. This delegation requested

[1] H.V. Seshadri (ed.), *Dr. Hedgewar, the Epoch-Maker: A Biography*, Bangalore: Sahitya Sindhu Prakashan, 1981, p. 61.
[2] Ibid., p. 71.

Doctorji that this movement will give independence and Sangh should not lag behind. At that time, when a gentleman told Doctorji that he was ready to go to jail, Doctorji said: 'Definitely go. But who will take care of your family then?' That gentleman replied, 'I have sufficiently arranged resources not only to run the family expenses for two years but also to pay fines according to the requirements.' Then Doctorji told him: 'If you have fully arranged for the resources then come out to work for the Sangh for two years.' After returning home that gentleman neither went to jail nor came out to work for the Sangh.[3]

The RSS remained loyal to the British till the end. Echoing the colonial state's stand on the Quit India Movement, Golwalkar says, 'After 1942, people often started thinking that there was no need to think of the law.'[4] He confessed that despite resentment among some RSS cadres, '[the] Sangh vowed not to do anything' in 1942.[5]

In fact, Golwalkar was not embarrassed at the RSS's loyalty to the British. In a speech in Indore in 1960, he said,

Many people worked with the inspiration to free the country by throwing the British out. . . . In fact there was no need to have this much inspiration. We should remember that in our pledge we have talked of the freedom of the country through defending religion and culture. There is no mention of departure of the British in that.[6]

He justified the principle 'Might is Right' with recourse to the idea of social Darwinism, which is not only scientifically bogus, but is also discredited for its connection with Nazism and other

[3] *Shri Guruji Samagra Darshan* (collected works of Golwalkar in Hindi; hereafter *SGSD*), vol. 4, pp. 39–40.

[4] Ibid., p. 41.

[5] Ibid., p. 40.

[6] Ibid., p. 2.

forms of racism. In a speech on June 8, 1942, when the Indian masses were facing massive repression, Golwalkar declared,

It is futile to blame the strong for the injustice done to the weak. Sangh does not want to waste its invaluable time in abusing or criticising others. If we know that large fish eat the smaller ones, it is outright madness to blame the big fish. Law of nature whether good or bad is true all the time. This rule does not change by terming it unjust.[7]

Golwalkar inherited this inimical attitude to the freedom struggle from his mentor and founder of the RSS, Hedgewar. The official biography of Hedgewar has the following telling statement: 'After establishing Sangh[,] Doctor Saheb in his speeches used to talk only of Hindu organisation. Direct comment on Government used to be nil.'[8]

DENIGRATION OF THE MARTYRDOM TRADITION

RSS literature discredits the tradition of martyrdom of our revolutionaries. Golwalkar declared that his objects of worship had always been successful personalities and that 'Bharatiya culture' (which means for the RSS only their version of Hindu culture) did not adore and idealize martyrdom or treat 'such martyrs as their heroes'. He says,

There is no doubt that such men who embrace martyrdom are great heroes and their philosophy too is pre-eminently manly. They are far above the average men who meekly submit to fate and remain

---

[7] *SGSD*, vol. 1, pp. 11–2.
[8] C.P. Bhishikar, *Sangh Vriksh Ke Beej: Dr. Keshavrao Hedgewar*, Delhi: Suruchi Prakashan, 1994, p. 24.

in fear and inaction. All the same, such persons are not held up as ideals in our society. We have not looked upon their martyrdom as the highest point of greatness to which man should aspire. For, after all, they failed in achieving their ideal, and failure implies some fatal flaw in them.[9]

Could there be a statement more insulting and denigrating to our martyrs than this? Golwalkar was, in fact, following Hedgewar in this respect. According to his biography published by the RSS, Hedgewar stressed that,

> Patriotism is not only going to prison. It is not correct to be carried away by such superficial patriotism. He used to urge that while remaining prepared to die for the country when the time came, it is very necessary to have a desire to live while organising for the freedom of the country.[10]

Surely, had Hedgewar come in contact with Bhagat Singh and his comrades, he would have termed them 'superficial patriots', and tried to dissuade them from their revolutionary path! But he didn't stir anywhere near any revolutionary, which is hardly surprising. After all, the whole of the RSS remained far away from the freedom struggle. Forget about producing martyrs, not a single important RSS functionary even went to jail for anti-colonial activities.

ALIGNING WITH THE MUSLIM LEAGUE

The RSS was not alone in betraying the anti-colonial movement in India. The author of *Hindutva* (1923) and Hedgewar's

---

[9] M.S. Golwalkar, *Bunch of Thoughts*, Bangalore: Sahitya Sindhu Prakashan, 1996, p. 283.

[10] Bhishikar, *Sangh Vriksh Ke Beej*, p. 21.

inspiration, Vinayak Damodar Savarkar, openly opposed and denigrated the freedom struggle. But that is not all. Savarkar's party, the Hindu Mahasabha, entered into an alliance with the Muslim League itself to wreck the unity of the freedom struggle. In 1942, in his presidential address to the 24th session of the Mahasabha at Kanpur, Savarkar said,

> In practical politics also the Mahasabha knows that we must advance through reasonable compromises. Witness the fact that only recently in Sind, the Sind-Hindu-Sabha on invitation had taken the responsibility of joining hands with the League itself in running [the] coalition Government. The case of Bengal is well known. Wild Leaguers whom even the Congress with all its submissiveness could not placate grew quite reasonably compromising and sociable [*sic*] as soon as they came in contact with the Hindu Mahasabha and the Coalition Government, under the premiership of Mr. Fazlul Huq and the able lead of our esteemed Mahasabha leader Dr. Syama Prasad Mookerji, functioned successfully for a year or so to the benefit of both the communities.[11]

## BACK-STABBING NETAJI SUBHAS CHANDRA BOSE

The RSS and its camp-followers express supposed admiration for Netaji Subhas Chandra Bose as a great freedom fighter. How sincere their admiration is can be judged by the fact that when Netaji was building the Indian National Army (Azad Hind Fauj) in foreign lands for a military campaign to force the British out, Savarkar, with the concurrence of RSS, joined hands with the British rulers. As president of the Hindu Mahasabha, he gave the following directive to the common Hindus of the country during his address to the 1941 Bhagalpur session of the party:

---

[11] Ibid., pp. 479–80.

So far as India's defence is concerned, Hindudom must ally unhesitatingly, in a spirit of responsive co-operation, with the war effort of the Indian government in so far as it is consistent with the Hindu interests, by joining the Army, Navy and the Aerial forces in as large a number as possible and by securing an entry into all ordnance, ammunition and war craft factories. . . . Hindu Mahasabhaites must, therefore, rouse Hindus especially in the provinces of Bengal and Assam as effectively as possible to enter the military forces of all arms without losing a single minute.[12]

This declaration of 'responsive co-operation' was put into action when Savarkar called upon Hindus 'to flood the [British] army, the navy and the aerial forces with millions of Hindu warriors with Hindu Sanghatanist hearts'.[13] Savarkar also informed the Mahasabha cadres that through the efforts of the Mahasabha alone, one lakh Hindus were recruited in the British armed forces in just one year.[14] It is important to note here that even the Muslim League, subservient to the British rulers, refused to organize such recruitment camps.

HATRED FOR SYMBOLS
OF COMPOSITE NATIONALISM

With a firm belief in the two-nation theory, it was natural for the RSS to despise the symbols of our united struggle and composite Indian nationalism. The RSS organ, *Organiser*, in its issue on the very eve of Independence, dated August 14, 1947, rejected the whole concept of a composite nation (under the editorial caption 'Whither'):

[12] V.D. Savarkar, *Samagra Savarkar Wangmaya: Hindu Rashtra Darshan*, vol. 6, Poona: Maharashtra Prantik Hindusabha, 1963, p. 460.
[13] Ibid., p. 461.
[14] Ibid., p. 439.

Let us no longer allow ourselves to be influenced by false notions of nationhood. . . . [I]n Hindusthan only the Hindus form the nation and the national structure must be built on that safe and sound foundation. . . . [T]he nation itself must be built up of Hindus, on Hindu traditions, culture, ideas and aspirations.

The Indian Tricolour as the National Flag, which represents an all-inclusive nationalism, was the target of special hatred for the Hindu nationalist. When the Indian Constituent Assembly adopted the Tricolour as the National Flag, the English organ of the RSS in its issue dated August 14, 1947, denigrated this choice by declaring that, despite the Congress rulers' decision, it would 'never be respected and owned by Hindus'; '[t]he word three is in itself an evil, and a flag having three colours will certainly produce a very bad psychological effect and is injurious to a country'.

BRAZEN LOVE FOR CASTEISM

What is the RSS alternative to a democratic-secular polity? They desire a Hindu *rashtra* where the *Manusmruti* would be law. The Constituent Assembly of India ratified the Constitution on November 26, 1949, and on November 30, *Organiser* editorially commented, 'But in our constitution there is no mention of the unique constitutional development in ancient Bharat. . . . But to our constitutional pundits that means nothing.' The *Manusmruti* is known for its derogatory and inhuman references to Shudras, Dalits, and women. It was for this reason that a copy of the *Manusmruti* was burnt as a protest in the presence of B.R. Ambedkar during the historic Mahad agitation (March 20, 1927).

For the RSS, there was no ambiguity regarding its 'national mission'. It was the enforcement of *Manusmruti* as the law of the land. The choice of *Manusmruti* was the outcome of the RSS's idealization of the *varna* system and caste society. According to the most prominent ideologue of the RSS—Golwalkar—the Hindu nation, Hindu nationalism and casteism are synonymous. He declared,

> The Hindu People [*sic*] . . . is the *Virat Purusha*, the Almighty manifesting Himself. Though they did not use the word 'Hindu', it is clear from the following description of the Almighty in *Purusha Sukta* wherein it is stated that sun and moon are His eyes, the stars and the skies are created from His *nabhi* (navel) and . . . *Brahmin is the head, Kshatriya the hands, Vaishya the thighs and Shudra the feet.* This means that the people who have this fourfold arrangement, i.e., the Hindu People, is [*sic*] our God. . . .
>
> This supreme vision of Godhead is the very core of our concept of 'nation' and has permeated our thinking and given rise to various unique concepts of our cultural heritage.[15]

Golwalkar was invited to address the students of the School of Social Sciences of Gujarat University on December 17, 1960. A decade after India adopted a Constitution that promised equal rights to all, irrespective of gender or caste or religion or region, Hindutva's preeminent guru defended the oppressive caste system:

> Today we try to run down the Varna system through ignorance. But it was through this system that a great effort to control possessiveness could be made. . . . In society some people are intellectuals, some are expert in production and earning of wealth and some have the capacity to labour. Our ancestors saw these four broad divisions in the society. The Varna system means nothing else but a proper co-ordination of these divisions and an enabling of the individual to serve the society to the best of his ability through a hereditary

---

[15] Golwalkar, *Bunch of Thoughts*, pp. 36–7. Italics in the original.

development of the functions for which he is best suited.[16]

The RSS claims to be working in the interest of all Hindus. This is a lie. It conceives of a Hindu society with Brahminical hegemony—the north Indian Brahminical vision at that. All Hindus are not equal; forget about Dalits, even high-caste Hindus of the south of India were considered racially inferior. In the same address at the Gujarat University, while underlying his firm belief in race theory, Golwalkar justifies a reprehensible practice where upper-caste men sexually exploited women:

> In an effort to better the human species through cross-breeding the Namboodri Brahamanas of the North were settled in Kerala and a rule was laid down that the eldest son of a Namboodri family could marry only the daughter of Vaishya, Kshatriya or Shudra communities of Kerala. Another still more courageous rule was that the first off-spring of a married woman of any class must be fathered by a Namboodri Brahman and then she could beget children by her husband. Today this experiment will be called adultery but it was not so, as it was limited to the first child.

Astonishingly, Golwalkar expressed these racist and anti-women views in the presence of the faculty and students of a prime university in Gujarat. The RSS, with its belief in the *Manusmruti*, naturally believed in inequality as the essence of Hindu society. Golwalkar hated democracy, which is the hallmark of the present RSS/BJP rulers too. While addressing 1,350 top-level cadres of the RSS at its headquarters at Nagpur in 1940, he declared, 'The RSS inspired by one flag, one leader and one ideology is lighting the flame of Hindutva in each and every corner of this great land.'[17]

---

[16] M.S. Golwalkar, cited in *Organiser*, January 2, 1961, pp. 5 and 16.
[17] *SGSD*, vol. 1, p. 11.

This slogan of 'one flag, one leader and one ideology' was directly borrowed from the programmes of the Nazi and Fascist parties of Europe.

HIDE-AND-SEEK WITH POLITICS

We often hear that the RSS is a cultural-social organization and has nothing to do with politics:

> The RSS is not a political party. It does not take part in elections, nor its office-bearers are supposed to become office-bearers of any political party. The RSS has no election symbol, nor its leadership or members have ever endeavoured to seek political office. It is a social-cultural organisation trying to inspire all national activity.[18]

We must compare this claim of the RSS with the following statement of Golwalkar which he made while addressing top-level cadres of the RSS at Indore on March 5, 1960:

> We know this also that some of our Swayamsevaks work in politics. There they have to organise according to the needs of work, public meetings, processions, etc., have to raise slogans. All these things have no place in our work. However, the actor should portray the character accepted to the best of his capability. But sometimes Swayamsevaks go beyond the role assigned to a performer (nat) as they develop over-zealousness in their hearts, to the extent that they become useless for this work. This is not good.[19]

We find here Golwalkar referring to the *swayamsevaks* loaned out to political offshoots as '*nat*', or performers, who are meant

[18] *Organiser*, Delhi, February 6, 2000.
[19] *SGSD*, vol. 4, pp. 4–5.

to dance to the tune of the RSS. One of the RSS publications titled *Param Vaibhav ke Path Par* ('On the Road to Great Glory') gives details of more than 40 organizations created by the RSS for different tasks and the BJP figures prominently at number four.[20] Professor Kasbe's work, which exposes the real face of the RSS and unearths its hidden agenda, was mirrored in the writings of one of the greatest socialist ideologues of India, Madhu Limaye, who also fought valiant ideological battles against the anti-national Hindutva ideology when the RSS was trying to take over the Janata Party in 1977–79.[21] Limaye, writing at around the same time (1979) as *Zot* was written, stated that 'our first difference with the RSS was over the issue of nationalism. We believed that every citizen had equal rights in the Indian nation. But the RSS and the Savarkarites came up with their notion of Hindu Rashtra'.

The second difference was that 'we dreamt of the birth of a democratic republic while the RSS claimed that democracy was a western concept that was not appropriate for India'. In those days, members of the RSS were full of praise for Adolf Hitler and agreed with Golwalkar that India must be cleansed of Muslims and Christians, as Hitler had done with the Jews in Germany. According to Golwalkar, 'Germany has also shown how well-nigh impossible it is for races and cultures having differences going to the root, to be assimilated into one united whole, a good lesson for us in Hindustan to learn and profit by.'[22]

According to Limaye, the other major difference with RSS was the latter's brazen defence of casteism making an indispensable part of Hinduism and the Hindu nation. Limaye wrote that 'Chanakya's *Arthashastra*, from which Guruji takes his inspiration,

---

[20] S.D. Sapre, *Param Vaibhav ke Path Par*, Delhi: Suruchi Prakashan, 1997, p. 7.

[21] Madhu Limaye, 'What is RSS?'. This tract was written soon after the split in the Janata Party, and was published in the Hindi weekly, *Ravivar*, in 1979.

[22] M.S. Golwalkar, *We or Our Nationhood Defined*, Nagpur: Bharat Publications, 1939, p. 35.

clearly states that it is the religious duty of the *Sudras* to serve the Brahmins, the *Kshatriyas* and the *Vaishyas*. In a clever subterfuge, Guruji replaces service of the upper castes with "service of society".

RSS made the first concerted attempt to capture the Indian state when the Janata Party government was in power at the Centre (1977–79). Publication of works like *Zot* at that juncture exposed the Hindutva camp's real intentions. The RSS did not succeed, but the Janata Party government did not survive either. Today, the Indian state is under total control of the RSS through its cadres. With its nefarious vision for India, it is not difficult to realize that this flag-bearer of Hindu nationalism, casteism and totalitarianism presents the greatest threat to the continuation of the democratic-secular polity of the country.

Dr. Ambedkar had warned against this danger in 1940 itself. According to him, 'If Hindu Raj does become a fact, it will, no doubt, be the greatest calamity for this country. . . . [It] is a menace to liberty, equality and fraternity. On that account it is incompatible with democracy. Hindu Raj must be prevented at any cost.'[23]

Publications like *Decoding the RSS* help equip ideologically all those who care to uphold the idea of an egalitarian India.

---

[23] B.R. Ambedkar, *Pakistan or the Partition of India*, Bombay: Government of Maharashtra, 1990, p. 358. First published in 1940.

# Decoding the RSS

It may be your interest
to be our masters,
but how can it be ours
to be your slaves?

—Thucydides

# PREFACE TO THE SEVENTH EDITION

Civilizations grow, [Carroll] Quigley argued in 1961, because they have an 'instrument of expansion', that is, a military, religious, political, or economic organization that accumulates surplus and invests it in productive innovations. Civilizations decline when they stop the 'application of surplus to new ways of doing things. In modern terms we say that the rate of investment decreases'. This happens because the social groups controlling the surplus have a vested interest in using it for 'nonproductive but ego-satisfying purposes . . . which distribute the surpluses to consumption but do not provide more effective methods of production'. People live off their capital and the civilization moves from the stage of the universal state to the stage of decay.

—Samuel Huntington, *Clash of Civilizations and the Remaking of World Order*[1]

My book, *Zot*—translated from Marathi into English as *Decoding the RSS: Its Tradition and Politics*—was first published in May 1978. Some enthusiastic activists of the Rashtriya Swayamsevak Sangh (RSS), or the Sangh, made a public bonfire of the book on June 9, 1978, in Pune, during a session of the Janata Party. They were also members of the Janata Party and they did not want the book to be sold at the party's programme. Socialist members of the party opposed the move, which led to a conflict

---

[1] Huntington citing from Carroll Quigley's *The Evolution of Civilizations: An Introduction to Historical Analysis*.

between the Socialists and RSS activists. The conflict contributed to the cracks that were already building within the Janata Party, which split soon after. All this brought the book into the limelight and its sale reached record numbers. The publisher had to produce three editions in a period of four months. The book went into several editions later and it was also translated into Kannada and Telugu.

## THE OBJECTIVES OF *ZOT*

Over forty years have passed since *Zot* was first published. A lot of water has flowed under the bridge since then. When it was published, the RSS was functioning as a pressure group and was allied with the Janata Party, which was in power then. Committed to its Hindutva ideology, the RSS aimed to work within that purview with its loyal and dynamic group of activists. Its second supremo, M.S. Golwalkar, had laid down an ideological framework for the RSS in his book, *Bunch of Thoughts*, which was published in 1966. The post-Emergency period saw a marked rise in right-wing forces, which organized gradually and became more powerful. They joined hands with the Janata Party after it was formed in 1977. These forces, especially the Sangh, cumulatively organized and empowered different groups and individuals to come to power. This was the main purpose of the Sangh's existence. So, when the Janata Party was to form the government at the centre, questions about its policies and the programmes it should implement obviously surfaced among the party members. *Zot* was written as a response to these questions. I confined my discussion to Golwalkar's book, *Bunch of Thoughts*—rather, its translation in Marathi, entitled *Vichardhan*. In other words, *Zot* is a criticism of *Bunch of Thoughts*. Just as several people acclaimed it, many had protested against it too. *Zot* became an object of severe criticism and the RSS activists who had not read Golwalkar's book were inspired to read it and understand its contents. I wished that besides the RSS members, others too would critically read *Bunch of Thoughts* and form their opinions about it.

A POWERFUL PRESSURE GROUP

It is true that due to imaginative strategies and implementation of different programmes of the RSS in the period between 1978 and 2003, the Bharatiya Janata Party's (BJP) journey to power became easier. Although the BJP is not in power now, it has had to adapt to its allies who are ideologically opposed to its line, and so it is drawn into an awkward situation. By giving up its principles, it has been making self-contradictory compromises. Obviously, the BJP is very disillusioned. The other organizations affiliated to the RSS, like Vishwa Hindu Parishad, Bajrang Dal, Bharatiya Mazdoor Sangh, Akhil Bharatiya Vidyarthi Parishad, Swadeshi Jagran Manch, etc. have frequently criticized the BJP. The criticism was aimed at pressurizing the BJP to implement their ideology. Despite criticizing the BJP, they often justified its actions and decisions. However, they took care to not be too severe in their criticism as they knew that it might lead to self-destruction. The Sangh used to claim that it was purely a cultural organization. But in 2002 it exposed itself when it demanded that its political affiliate, the BJP, take a decision on dividing Kashmir into three parts. This surprised everyone. It then contested the elections in Kashmir representing its ideology.[2] This established the fact that the RSS is not a cultural

---

[2] The RSS came into conflict with the BJP ahead of the 2002 Jammu and Kashmir assembly election, when it blamed the BJP-led union government for not doing enough to rehabilitate Kashmiri Pandits. The RSS demanded trifurcation of the state—with Jammu as a separate state and Ladakh as a union territory—which the BJP termed 'anti-national'. The RSS backed the Jammu State Morcha in the election, which fielded 12 candidates contesting on the plank of separate statehood for Jammu. None of them won.

organization; it is a powerful political pressure group in spirit.

## PROTECTORS OF THE CHATURVARNYA TRADITION

We understand the true nature of the Sangh when we examine its style of working since its inception and, similarly, the strategies it has adopted from time to time. More and more, it would gradually come to light and become apparent to us. Since its establishment in 1925, the RSS has used a different language to claim that the work it has been engaged in is unique. The organization's basic principles— its highly held values—are cultural nationalism, religious absolutism and patriotism. It believes that a nation can progress only with these principles and values. The Sangh's views are very different from others' and it promotes them for a unique form of nation-building and construction of national life. The main track, of nation-building, is to give the country the status of a mother, hence the term 'Bharat Mata'. The founder of the RSS, Dr. Keshav Baliram Hedgewar often said, 'Love is a means to connect people.' But what is the path to achieve this objective? What are the action-based programmes to achieve the aims? Hedgewar never explained it. So, there is a sense of uncertainty and hesitancy among the Sangh's activists about its objectives and strategies. A number of former *swayamsevaks* have recorded this. However, the RSS activists can tell you this much about the Sangh, which is the only thing they are certain about: the RSS is an organization of Hindus.

Several important political events took place in the first 25 years (1925–50) of the Sangh's existence. The organization was established in Nagpur, and the communal riots of 1927 were a precursor to what followed. There is enough information to point to the fact that when the Hindu–Muslim riots took place, the Sangh as an organization was used to mobilize Hindus against the Muslims. There was a considerable rise in the membership of the RSS as the riots progressively worsened. In other words, the Sangh satisfied the urge among Hindus to form an opposition to resist the organized communalism of Muslims in India. When the Simon Commission came to India in 1928 to look at constitutional reforms, the entire country protested against it, and several organizations fighting for freedom displayed black flags. Under pressure from the working class, the Congress had to pass a resolution demanding '*poorna swaraj*' (complete freedom) in 1929. The Congress decided to observe January 26 as Independence Day from the following year. The Dandi March in 1930 and Quit India Movement in 1942 were important political events during the freedom movement. However, the Sangh did not participate in any of these events, and it never explained its reasons for not doing so. The Indian Independence movement progressed under the leadership of the Indian National Congress. One reason for the Sangh to remain away from political events during the freedom movement could have been that it did not wish to follow the Congress, which was leading the movement, because it was founded by a British civil servant, A.O. Hume. Equally, the Sangh was wary of Vinayak Damodar Savarkar and his organization, Hindu Mahasabha. In 1939, Hindus faced injustice under the Nizam's rule in Hyderabad, and Savarkar led protests in Hyderabad. The Sangh should have taken part in this protest, to at least organize the Hindus, but that did not happen. Why?

Many people participated in the freedom movement and became martyrs, but the Sangh said, 'All this blood is wasted; the country is not yet prepared for freedom.' (S.H. Deshpande, who was once an ardent follower of the RSS, has recorded this.) The RSS was criticized by many for not participating in the freedom movement, but it ignored the criticism. Did the Sangh, which is interested in organizing Hindus, at least oppose the partition of their very dear motherland? This did not happen either. Savarkar's biographer, Dhananjay Keer, has made important observations in this regard:

> The RSS remained mere passive spectators and refused co-operation, official or otherwise, to the Hindu Mahasabha even in peaceful demonstrations against the vivisection of the Motherland, as if nothing had happened in the life of the nation to which they pledged their blood, brains and bones morning, noon and night. A little later they went to jail; not for opposing the vivisection of their Motherland, but for protesting against the ban on their organisation.[3]

Why was the Sangh not interested in the freedom movement? One should examine this carefully and find answers. In my view, the reasons lie in the Sangh's tradition of safeguarding the Chaturvarnya system. The political philosophy of ancient India, from the period of the *Mahabharata's Shanti Parva* ('Book of Peace') to Chanakya's *Arthashastra* ('Treatise on Economics'), protects Chaturvarnya. In ancient India, the main duty of a king, a Kshatriya, was to protect tradition, and the king who did not perform his duty would be humiliated. There grew an intimate relationship between the king and the Chaturvarnya system because of this. The inevitable impact of the tradition was that it completely neglected the real role of a king. He was not required to have any special administrative abilities and was only expected to respect the tradition—he could be anyone as long as he respected this tradition. The Brahmins would admire him and please him if he played his part. This tradition was not opposed during the Shaka and Kushana eras, nor during the era of Muslim rulers and the British. But the kings who rejected the Chaturvarnya tradition were opposed. The defeats faced by India, its enslavement, and the resistance to debate, are rooted in the sustenance of this tradition.

---

[3] Dhananjay Keer, *Veer Savarkar*, Mumbai: Popular Prakashan, 1966, p. 388.

It seems to me that from ancient times to the arrival of the British in India, the intellectualism of the Brahmin class, which was always placed at the pinnacle of society, was spent justifying the Chaturvarnya tradition—and the Kshatriyas spent all their power in implementing the tradition. This appears to be the major reason for India's backwardness. It was only after these dominating classes gradually freed themselves from the restrictive Chaturvarnya ideology that they were able to achieve some success in other fields. And when they were freed from their narrow attitudes, the Bahujan communities were also unchained and empowered to show their aptitude in varied fields. If the Chaturvarnya system had continued as it was, Indians would not have flowered in the Silicon Valley of America, and Bangalore would not have been an important city of modern technology. So, before we ask why the RSS did not participate in the freedom movement of India, we have to understand the tradition that the organization represents.

## THE GOLWALKARIAN INTERPRETATION
## OF *GUNA* AND *KARMA*

Golwalkar never disguised his admiration for ancient tradition. He was proud of it and made efforts to propagate it throughout his life. Once, in the 1960s, he was asked to explain the meaning of the Chaturvarnya system—whether it was a tradition or a religion. Golwalkar replied that it is not a tradition but a religion. He said, the *shrutis* and *smrutis* are the creations of God, and Chaturvarnya, which is a part of them, is also from a divine scheme. Nevertheless, he added, we need not worry if it became distorted, because even if man dismantled it, it would re-establish itself as it is a God-given structure. Golwalkar was asked another question: was Chaturvarnya based on *guna* (character) and *karma* (conduct) or the actual life lived by an individual?

The answer postulated by Golwalkar is unambiguous. He said, it is true that Chaturvarnya is *guna* and *karma*, and while *guna* indicates aptitude, *karma* is the occupation chosen by oneself. But, continued Golwalkar, this interpretation of the terms, *guna* and *karma*, is incorrect. He explained, *guna* is nature, which comprises *satva* (essence), *rajas* (passion), and *tamas* (ignorance), and *karma* refers to your actions in your past life. You obtain *varna* in the present life as per your *karma* of the previous life, said Golwalkar. Numerous illustrations from Golwalkar's writings and speeches can be cited to show his conviction that Chaturvarnya was God's creation and that our present is a derivative of our past life. They have been cited in some of my other writings, so I do not wish to reproduce them here. The point is that it was Golwalkar's dream to sustain Chaturvarnya without any impediments. This is also the chief objective of the RSS. The organization envisions creating leaders who are like the kings of ancient or medieval times, who can protect this system and who will uphold political power in the country. It wants to produce a consensus in society with the support of religious sentiments.

The major nemeses of the Sangh have been discussed extensively in *Zot*. They are: Islam, Christianity and Communism. These three ideologies oppose Chaturvarnya. An important meeting of the Sangh was organized in Bangalore in March 2001, where a three-pronged programme for the Indian Muslim communities was declared by M.G. Vaidya, the Sangh's official spokesperson.[4] One of the demands laid down at the meeting was that the Muslim community should reframe some of the Islamic concepts, like *kafir* and *jihad*, and that they should take care to avoid being trapped by sham Hindu leaders. On the contrary, they were told, they must strengthen liberal Muslim thinkers like Asghar Ali Engineer, Sikander Bakht and Mushirul Hasan. It was

---

[4] *Maharashtra Times*, March 29, 2001.

also demanded that if violence was perpetrated against Hindus anywhere in the world, the Muslims of India must protest against it. The mention of Engineer's name by Vaidya was indeed a shock to everyone because Engineer is a leading Marxist thinker of India. Perhaps Vaidya was not familiar with his writings. Liberal secular Hindus are also included in the list of the Sangh's opponents. Although a list of foes existed before too, at the meeting the mention of liberal secular Hindus was underlined with a certain degree of emphasis. In other words, it was sharpened a little more.

The Hindu–Muslim question is not a new one to Indians; it has a long tradition in Indian history. But, in the last ten to fifteen years this discussion has become fierce and vicious. Muslim fundamentalists and Hindu communalists are comparatively few in number in India. However, due to the wealth they possess and the organized power they can harness, they have engulfed the entire population of the country. The majority of people in both the communities are not fundamentalist or communal, and both communities have substantially contributed to the social, political and cultural spheres and to the development of the country. In spite of this, why did the two pressure groups become so influential? Why do both groups stand together in opposition to secular forces? It is possible for us to discover a reliable answer to this question in this inquiry.

A SHARED DISEASE: HINDU COMMUNALISM
AND MUSLIM FUNDAMENTALISM

Hindu religion is an ancient religion. Its Vedic culture is unique as compared to other cultures in the world. In the socio-cultural history of ancient India, Vedic culture played an important role, when there were no caste traditions in Indian society. The process of caste creation and the determination of caste by birth had not yet begun. Like all cultures of the world, it had several flaws too, but the religion had profound insight to develop the varied dimensions of life. It provided the world with a precious gift in the form of Upanishadic philosophy. It produced epics like the *Ramayana* and *Mahabharata*, and geniuses like Bhasa and Kalidasa. It created scientists like Aryabhatta and Charaka. India's contributions are enchanting in the sphere of the arts, such as dance and sculpture. Later, Buddha's and Mahavira's philosophies developed this culture to a great extent, and subsequently it was transformed into a composite form called 'Indian culture'. This culture, therefore, remained distinguished for a long period of time in the world. But its all-inclusive and broad character did not last for long because of internal clashes among groups that were in conflict with one another. In due course of time, the ancient Vedic culture became Hindu culture and the misconception that this Hindu culture was a superior one was circulated all over the world.

Once you consider yourselves the most superior community in the world, and that yours is the greatest culture in the world, you are infected by a disease called narcissism. This is a disease of self-gratification. This mental disorder leads to such irrationality that an infected patient is not aware of the changes and transformation in their cultural environment. The world changes and it keeps changing; social reality, culture and man develop. But this narcissist is not prepared to accept the changes.

There were several foreign invasions, and the outsiders taught us innumerable new things. Many of them intermingled with us without much difficulty. But some of them meticulously retained their identities. Muslim rulers ruled over this country for more than five hundred years. They provided us with a new governing system and made enormous efforts to increase agricultural produce and income. Lakhs of Indians were invited to convert to Islam. On this basis, their power increased. The Hindus were powerless to fight the Muslim conquerors because they were engrossed in themselves and immersed in their admiration of Hindu culture's superiority. They did not acquire the skills, competencies and abilities that were needed for social development and the progress of their nation. In the changing times, several things became outdated. But they could not comprehend them due to their egoistic attitude and narcissistic temperament, which they could not give up. On the other hand, Islamic culture was novel to the Hindus. It was a culture that had the resolve to achieve newer things. It earned the distinction of being the bravest culture in the world. One of the effects of Islamic culture in India was its political domination, which lasted long.

Cultural superiority and the pride that it imbued in the Hindus disrupted their interactions with the world. Consequently, the various skills, arts, science, technology and modernity acquired by the rest of the world were never produced in the Hindu consciousness. So they remained regressive, ignorant, confined to their spaces, and defeated. They had a progressive leader like Savarkar, who introduced modernity to them, but it was too late for them to improve. Besides, they completely disapproved of what Savarkar was telling them, and continued without any compromise. They disapproved of his modern views, scientific convictions and utilitarian thoughts. On the contrary, they made as much fun of Savarkar as they could. The world was changing, there were enormous social transformations, and several new political powers had assumed new roles. However, the Hindus contributed little to this transformation because they had little to do with the changing reality. They were nostalgic and busy visualizing hollow dreams of the future. Even today, they have not been able to come out of this nostalgic straitjacket.

The history of Muslims followed a similar trajectory. Since its rise in medieval times until its fall, Islam spread in the world along progressive lines, both politically and culturally. From the seventh century onwards, Muslim armies invaded Syria, Palestine, Egypt and North Africa, and Christians in these countries were converted to Islam. In the eighth century, the Muslims invaded Spain and Portugal and attacked France. In the ninth century, they invaded Sicily and attacked the mainland of Italy. Later, India as well as China were invaded. The Muslims not only had a progressive army but they were also an advanced economic power. They were involved in mercantile transactions across continents, in Asia, Europe and Africa. They bought gold and slaves from Africa, wool from Europe, and in exchange sold spices and other products from Asia. They sold paper produced in China to other parts of the world. Muslims took the numeral system invented in India to the world, and it became the basis for scientific progress all over the globe. They cultivated the sciences and the arts, and built upon the knowledge systems and scholarship of ancient western Asia and Greece. They were at the forefront in the domains of science and culture during the medieval period. Europe was able to transform itself by translating the knowledge acquired by the Muslims. At that time, Muslims were like gurus, and Europe appeared to be their newly admitted student.

However, the Muslims became narcissists and, like the Hindus, their cultural superiority and egotism caused them to become engrossed in self-glorification and self-gratification. They believed that Muslims were superior and the only civilized and powerful people in the world—and that those living in the regions outside Islamic control were 'kafirs', or infidels, and barbaric. Thus, they lived in a self-ruminating world and found solace in ridiculing non-Islamic people. They became so self-obsessed that they failed to note the transformations taking place in Europe at the end of the medieval era. The Renaissance and the Reformation movements in sixteenth-century Europe changed the world. It gave birth to a new human consciousness, a new culture, a new system of rules and a new economic system. The old world was dissolved and it ceased to exist. Martin Luther wrote the *Ninety-five Theses* on Indulgences criticizing the Catholic Church in Wittenburg, Germany. On the ceiling of the Sistine Chapel, in *The Creation of Adam*, Michelangelo painted God within the reach of man. Human beings became the centre of the universe, unsuppressed by religion and the priest. The regions that were conquered by the Muslims were freed from their control. But even then, Muslims were engrossed in their own egotistic meditation. Self-flattering Hindus and Muslims were both absorbed in their egotism.

In such a cultural scenario, it became easy for the British to invade India. Even after the arrival of the British, both Hindus and Muslims retained the same mood and state of mind. They came together and fought against the British only once, in 1857, during the 'Sepoy Mutiny' (described by freedom fighters as the First War of Independence). The unity of these two communities occurred only once in history. However, they could not fight the British because the colonial power was advanced from every point of view. They had brought with them the essence of the Renaissance and Reformation to India, and they were well equipped with weapons produced by modern science and technology. Defeating the communal Hindus and fundamentalist Muslims was easy as their minds were against modernity, modern science and technology, and modern human values. Though the two groups were enemies of each other, they both spoke against modernity, modern human values, and modern technology and science.

The resistance of Hindu communalism and Muslim fundamentalism had the same source. Even today they live in the ancient and medieval periods and their self-absorption has made them passive. Their ability to search for new domains and worlds has been annihilated. The majority of people all over the world have rejected religious fanaticism. They have embraced future prospects, physical advancements and revolutionary cultural paradigms. But these two groups remain where they were, haunted by feelings of inferiority. A person suffering from inferiority always seeks others' attention. By fighting amongst themselves and killing innocent people, Hindu communalists and Muslim fundamentalists are trying to attract attention towards themselves. If they feel proud for such killings, it is in reality a perversion caused by an inferior consciousness. The common people, farmers, the working class and the middle class of both communities must look for a way out of this perversion and fanaticism. Otherwise, their lives will be at stake and they won't make any progress in the physical and cultural spheres.

ATTITUDES TOWARDS MODERNITY

In today's world, people have accepted modern values for the enrichment of life and they aim to lead a civilized life. We must build social and political institutions on the basis of such values. In order to live an enriched and civilized life, we have embraced political democracy that represents ideals such as liberty, equality, fraternity and social justice. In our social life, we have promoted the principles of social welfare and secularism. In the economic sphere, some people have accepted the democratic socialist system, some have embraced the capitalist system and others have accepted the neo-capitalist system emerging from globalization. One cannot claim that any of these systems are flawless. But modern values like individual freedom, respect for other religions, fixing the boundaries of religion and politics, acceptance of science and the use of technology for physical progress—these are the important reference points. Hindu and Muslim communalists in India do not accept such principles simply because the West discovered or invented them. The West followed these principles and made enormous progress, and also taught us several things. Aided by inventions in science and technology, societies in the West are equipped with advanced weapons. Despite the fact that the Hindus and the Muslims were enemies of each other, once upon a time they had each promoted modernity, modern human values, science and technology. In the West, when people began to critically review religious texts such as the Bible in the light of modern science, religious leaders harassed them. In several instances, they were punished by death or literally burnt alive. In spite of such penalization and harassment, they did not refuse to embrace science. Instead, without disturbing its content, essence and convictions, they modernized their religion. A categorical line was drawn between political and religious powers, separating the two domains. Therefore, democracy and secularism survived and developed in Western societies, and they were able to make rapid progress. It docs not imply that people in Western societies embraced these principles entirely; several orthodox people exist there too. However, the societies were successful in alienating a minority group of the orthodox from the majority who believed in modernism.

Muslim and Hindu societies also made rapid progress in the past with the help of modern principles. But, each time, the orthodox produced several barriers in the name of religion. The orthodox Muslim world, instead of modernizing religion, started Islamizing modernity. With the power of wealth and the means of devastation that they possessed, the orthodox produced feelings of panic and fear in the minds of the common Muslims. But the claim that the entire Muslim world is against modernity and is prepared to perform *jihad* in the name of religion is part of anti-Muslim propaganda. After Taliban's rule was overthrown and defeated by the common Muslims in Afghanistan, numerous women in the country gave up their *burqa* (veil). There were long queues of men in front of barbers' shops to get shaved. The people on the streets demanded that Indian films be screened in theatres and that there be public performances of dance and music. The events were telecast as newsflash and were enthusiastically broadcast by the media on Indian TV screens. These were signs that Muslims remained enormously interested in modernity. However, after the Shah of Iran had ushered in modernity in his country, Ayatollah Khomeini seized power and annulled it along with the social development that the Shah had introduced.

In this context, are Golwalkar's views taking us into the future or are they taking us back to ancient India? Like Muslims demonstrating avowed faith in the Ummah, the worldwide Muslim community, Hindus too thought of organizing themselves along similar lines. Hence, Golwalkar founded the Vishwa Hindu Parishad (VHP) in 1964. After its establishment, a 'World Conference' of the Parishad was organized at Prayag during the religious festival of *Kumbhmela*. While addressing the conference, Golwalkar said,

On several occasions, people say that this age is the age of science. So they often argue that we have to bring about changes in religion in order to adapt to the age of science. I say exactly the opposite thing. I say that science must interface religion and bring about changes in it. If you go on changing religion with every research in science, then the religion will not remain religion. And if there would not be religion, then how would social life exist. Consequently, duties of people will be disturbed. The earthly and heavenly ways of welfare for people will be lost. The entire mankind will be then disenchanted. Hence, I think that to bring changes in religion with every research in science is not an appropriate way.[5]

---

[5] *Shri Guruji Samagra Darshan*, vol. 5, Nagpur: Bharatiya Vichardhara, 1975, p. 75.

The language used by Guruji is similar to that of the Muslims who want to Islamize modernity. Golwalkar wants to Saffronize modernity.

AGAINST MODERN VALUES

The revolutionary, Bhai Paramanand, established a Hindu–Communist Group in Punjab. His action is the best illustration of the Hindu community's response to modern political ideology. But Golwalkar severely criticized the formation of such a group, and said, 'A person can either be a Hindu or a Communist. He cannot be both.'[6]

Maulana Maududi also subscribed to the same view. He wrote,

In the context of my life, as long as I accept the ideology of Islam, I am a Muslim; but by accepting some other ideology, if I call myself a Muslim, then it would be ridiculous. Expressions such as 'Muslim Nationalist', 'Muslim Communist' would be like 'Communist Fascist', 'Communist Capitalist' or 'Holy Prostitute' and they would be obviously self-contradictory expressions.[7]

This implies that Hindu and Muslim fundamentalists of India speak the same language and oppose modern science and modern values of life. They both want to retain the purity of their religions. Besides, they want to revive the conditions that existed when their religions were born. Muslims do not subscribe to nationalism because Islamic beliefs are based on the concept of religious cosmology. Golwalkar, who advocated cultural nationalism, rebuked the 'territorial concept of nationalism', which according to

---

[6] M.S. Golwalkar, *Bunch of Thoughts*, Bangalore: Sahitya Sindhu Prakashan, 1996, p. 59. First published 1966.

[7] Sayyid Abulala Maududi, *Nationalism and India*, New Delhi, 1965, p. 8.

him was promoted by Congress leaders, and called it an absurdity.

The resolutions passed by the VHP at a conference held on April 7–8, 1984, at Vigyan Bhavan in New Delhi, are noteworthy. They were approved by the Dharma Sansad (literally, 'religious parliament') and published as 'Code of Conduct'. The first principle of the code states that villagers must build a temple in each village and they must congregate there at least twice a day. The second principle is that when saints, *rushis* or wise men visit a village, programmes should be organized in schools or at any other convenient place in the village. The third prescribes that after considering the suitability of the existing conditions, people must be trained in some religious rites and observances of orthodox rituals. The tenth principle is a religious decree that if a Hindu is converted to another religion, and if he wished to return to the Hindu religion, he may be allowed to come back only to his original caste. Finally, prayers are to be offered to the high priest. The sixth insists on the third *ashrama*, i.e. *vanaprasthashrama*, and says, 'The Chaturvarnya system must be established in such a way that from Acharya's vision no piece of land must slip away.'[8] It shows clearly where the Hindu and Muslim fundamentalists wish to take the nation. But in which direction is the nation really moving?

COMMUNAL ROADMAP FOR THE NATION

Our nation has been affected by unprecedented communal politics in contemporary times. Hindu communalists and Muslim fundamentalists point their fingers at each other. The riots generated on account of the demolition of Babri Masjid took us back by several years. The coordinated bomb explosions in Mumbai

---

[8] Sudhir Panse, *Ase Asel Hindu Rashtra* ('Such would be the Hindu Nation'), Mumbai: Lokvangmay, 1993.

produced a permanent loss of trust between the communities and generated ill feelings against each other. The Supreme Court verdict in the Shah Bano case led to a knee-jerk reaction from the Indian Parliament. The Parliament overturned the decision of the Supreme Court of India, and the Muslim Women (Protection of Rights on Divorce) Act, 1986 passed by it became a major bone of contention. This step followed the orthodox Muslim line of thinking. Naturally, the government's action caused disturbances across the nation. The Act may have been declared as progressive, but the decision of the Supreme Court was phenomenal. It was particularly significant in the context of Hindu–Muslim relations in India. The court's decision was important, given the guidelines in the Constitution for the formulation of a Uniform Civil Code. However, Rajiv Gandhi succumbed to the pressure of the orthodox Muslims' fundamentalism. Thus, from there on, not only did the nation's mainstream politics take a different turn, but it was completely overrun by communal ideologies.

In 1979, Dalits in Tamil Nadu converted to Islam, which gave more teeth to the VHP. When the decision on the Shah Bano case was diluted, Congress's power collapsed. In 1990, when, terrified by terrorist attacks, the Pandits began fleeing Kashmir, they could not be saved by Prime Minister V.P. Singh, or by Prime Minister Atal Bihari Vajpayee later. Hence, the feeling that the majority of Hindus were not safe and that they had been deprived in this country became stronger among the Hindu community. Insecurity in any human society makes people antagonistic and violent. How can Hindus be an exception to it? The aggression of Hindus increased in the country and, in 1998, Graham Staines, a Christian missionary, was burnt to death along with his two sons. In 2002, there was a terrifying and dreadful massacre of Hindus in Gujarat and it was followed by an organized and systematic massacre of Muslims. The livelihoods of Muslims were destroyed and their businesses were burnt to ashes. Muslim terrorists replied to the massacre by gunning down more than fifty people at the Akshardham Temple in Ahmedabad on September 24, 2002. It was like a chain of revenge between the communal Hindus and the fundamentalist Muslims. The length of this communal chain is increasing day by day and, as a result, the integrity of the nation is being viciously affected. If this chain is not disrupted immediately, poor young men from Hindu and Muslim families will fight among themselves and they will either die or waste away their lives. If you lengthen the chain of violence, there is the possibility that one group will achieve victory. Undoubtedly, however, more such attacks on each other will put the country's political stability at stake. This source of menace is risky for the nation's progress and it will bring the developmental processes of the nation to a halt as well.

Religion is an important psychological need of human beings, without which we feel unsafe. Such a sense of fear reduces us to helplessness. When the individual man became aware of his limitations, from that juncture he turned to religion for psychological support. We must understand the significant position of religion in the life of man and reflect on it. Crores of people believe that the journey of man's soul can achieve solace with the support of religion, and that religion can be a means to salvation. If religion is used for such intent and purpose, it can be a constructive force in the life of an individual. But when that is not the case, it can be a force of doom and devastation. However, religion is being expressed in extreme and dreadful forms in India today.

CADRE OF PROFESSIONAL RIOTERS

Several complex issues in India have remained unresolved. There are about thirty-five crore illiterate men and women in our country. About ten crore young people do not have safe employment. Small-scale farmers are working in difficult situations and they are not able to generate enough income from agricultural produce. In the industrial sector, due to economic depression, the intensity of unemployment is increasing beyond imagination. A diametrically opposite and ironical situation is growing: educated young men are raring to work for a notorious knave called Arun Gawli. If riots and violence keep growing, the phenomenon will produce professional riot-makers. To sustain their profession, they will ensure that riots occur regularly. The middle class in our country, which is approximately composed of around twenty crore people, does not have a clear idea of the impending menace. It harbours the notion that religious groups will protect it. But everyone suffers when riots become a profession. Several people think that a reliable solution to the issue will be found, but each of them is living under tremendous pressure. Only when the common people use their power to resist and alienate the riot-makers of both the communities can a solution be found. There is nothing wrong in expressing such hope because the human race has ridden along difficult roads since ancient times before reaching this stage. So it can certainly fight against any difficulty it might encounter in the future.

OBJECTIVES FOR THE FUTURE

Every nation in the world is preparing to welcome the new system of globalization. We have not been able to see the effects of globalization as was expected. Although both Hindu and Muslim communalists think of their social systems as being great and unique, they have become outdated in producing expansive development in the modern world. Unfortunately, the communalists are not paying attention to the modern world, because, as pointed out earlier, they are suffering from the diseases of self-gratification and self-glorification due to their cultural misconceptions. They are not in a position to understand that the world has gone ahead of them. Today, every action by India and Pakistan has to meet the approval of the United States. The World Bank (WB), International Trade Organization (ITO), International Monetary Fund (IMF) and such powerful and influential organizations are controlled by the US. India's dependence on these institutions is increasing by the day. But the communalists, who hide their inferiorities and go around killing people to prove their valour, are in fact cowardly and fear-stricken. How are they going to encounter globalization, which requires their valour and bravery?

In order to resolve the fundamental questions for Indians caught in the vortex of globalization, it is important to understand how the advanced nations of the world force us to work. How Indians move along by avoiding what is harmful is an important matter of consideration, because this parameter will determine how we evaluate our work. Globalization arrived in India on its own, not after consulting the Indian government nor the Hindus and Muslims in the country. In essence, its nature and form are non-political. Technology, capital and corporate managements are bringing the whole world closer. But the Hindu and Muslim fundamentalists of our country are counting the dead among young activists on the other side. Perhaps they are also measuring the increasing distance between Hindus and Muslims. This is obviously terrible from the point of view of the development and progress of Indian citizens. So, this is a crucial time for both Hindu and Muslim fundamentalists to shed their egotistic psyche. They must comprehend the reality and facts, and must know what is happening in the world. They must also make progress in their respective fields and compete with the rest. This will free them from their inferiority complex and, subsequently, each will require the other for the development of the nation. Every one of us, I feel, has to make efforts to achieve this objective.

Raosaheb Kasbe
2004

# 1. THE FOUNDATIONS OF THE RSS

Dr. Keshav Baliram Hedgewar founded the Rashtriya Swayamsevak Sangh (RSS) on the occasion of the Dasara festival in 1925. The organization's ideology and purpose were not elucidated at the time, and so its intentions were not clear. Besides, it appears that its members did not feel the need for an ideological framework. Perhaps because the country was in the throes of the Independence movement, the new organization passed off as one among many that were working to achieve freedom.

The founding members of RSS, or the Sangh, succeeded in establishing an organization by appealing to emotions. The intellectuals of the Sangh propagated ideas such as: 'The saffron flag is the nation's flag'; 'Hindustan is a country of Hindus'; and 'Ekachalakanuvartitva' (the principle of unquestioned submission to the authority of one leader). 'Discipline' was accorded the highest importance in the Sangh, which looked up to Nazi Germany and Fascist Italy as its ideals. However, the Sangh built its intellectual tradition through other means: by glorifying the history of Hindus; ridiculing democracy and democratic methods of functioning; and, by accusing and insulting the Indian National Congress. Many among those who have spent several years in the Sangh have recorded these strategies.[1] It was natural for the Sangh to feel that healthy discussions and debates on secularism, political national-

---

[1] For example, S.H. Deshpande in 'Sanghatale Diwas' (Days Spent in the Sangh), an essay published in *Mauj Diwali Ank*, 1974, a popular annual Marathi periodical.

ism and democracy were unrealistic and unnecessary, because neither did it believe in these principles nor in the Congress.

There is not much literature available to study the Sangh even today. After Hedgewar's death in 1940, Madhav Sadashiv Golwalkar, or Shri Guruji as he is known, took over the leadership of the RSS. His speeches and ideas delivered at various times have been compiled in *Bunch of Thoughts*,[2] which was first published in 1966. The members of the Sangh now consider the ideas recorded in this book to be their *yuga dharma* (the rules for daily life specific to this epoch). They believe that Golwalkar's thoughts are perfect and constructive. As much as the orthodox consider the Bible or the Quran to be the standard text, so does the Sangh consider *Bunch of Thoughts* to be the organization's doctrine. That is why it is necessary to discuss and critically analyse the book. Although not a difficult task, it is a time-consuming one, which has to be undertaken in order to understand the purpose and objectives of the RSS. Seeking clarity on the meaning and intentions of such an organization is necessary, for, without properly knowing it, merely accusing the Sangh would be inappropriate. Also, our expectations of the organization would be invalid if we didn't understand it.

Several ideologies have emerged all over the world in modern times, which have helped us understand and, subsequently, discuss the interrelationships between the individual and society. These ideologies have enhanced our perceptions of social, economic and political equality necessary for the development and enrichment of an individual. Many countries have embraced modern ideologies like democracy, socialism and communism in the belief that nations must be built on the principles of social justice and equality. Moreover, these ideologies, which although differ on many details, believe that international cooperation cannot be achieved unless countries are free of exploitation. It is through

---

[2] Golwalkar, *Bunch of Thoughts.*

such mutual understanding that the dream of a global state may become a reality some day.

However, Golwalkar disagrees with these modern ideologies. According to him, nationalist thought is natural in human beings. He says, any ideology, thought or an 'ism' that has its origin in a foreign nation cannot resolve the problems of India. He fervently attacks them, and writes,

> We stand for a harmonious synthesis among nations and not their obliteration. Needless to say, the idea of a stateless condition levelling all human beings to one particular plane of physical existence, erasing their individual and group traits, is foreign to us. The World State of our concept will, therefore, evolve out of a federation of autonomous and self-constrained nations under a common centre linking them all.

It suggests that whatever is unrelated to or inconsistent with the Indian Hindu traditions should not be accepted. While saying so, Golwalkar explains it clearly and without any ambiguity that a significant feature of Indian culture is economic inequality and the unequal physical existence of its people. In his opinion, we need to understand the basis of physical existence in the national and international contexts of the human community—how else can we protect its individual and collective peculiarities? But we must consider these questions from different perspectives. According to the ideologies of democracy, communism and socialism, unless we bring all groups of individuals on an equal physical plane, the properties of personal and collective characteristics are not protected and the opportunities for personal development are also not availed.

Golwalkar's speeches are likeable and attractive. Young people are easily taken in by his linguistic flourish and sensational depiction of our history. He refers to history so much that those among the young who have a deep interest in it get carried away by his accounts of the past. As a result, they don't exactly understand his premise, and so cannot examine the worthlessness of his speeches and the illogical connections he makes in them. In fact, the Sangh's young *swayamsevaks*, or volunteers, are usually at a formative stage of their lives, and naïve. It is not possible for them to understand the complexities of those speeches. But, when the convolutions become apparent at a later stage in their lives, time would have slipped from their grasp. They would only experience irritation, mental torture and defeatism. Although the RSS succeeded in building up an organization of energetic young people, it gave birth to a cursed generation that was seized by regret at a later stage of life.

According to Golwalkar's argument, if the human community progressed on equal material existence, its individualistic and collective features would be destroyed. Completely illogical, this argument is equally harmful to the dream of constructing a socialistic society. When we build a society on an unequal material basis, the power and means of production are concentrated in the hands of a particular class or caste that become the private owners of the entire structure. In order to maintain its hegemony, the powerful class will doggedly exploit the common people. This would be the principal reason to create an unequal material basis in society. In such a society, the rich enslave the workers, the landless labourers and the poor. What must the innumerable slaves do for the society to maintain its distinct and individualistic character? It follows that the enslaved must stay mute and in the dark, in the assumption that their suffering, poverty and humiliation are sins of their previous births, and that they must continue to sincerely work to produce wealth and power, and also allow the entire production system to remain in the hands of their respective masters! Golwalkar justifies the unequal material basis on which Hindu society stands. According to him, Hindu culture is a unique product of Hindu society, and he overwhelmingly favours the unequal system. In such a social system, the rich remain rich, or, at times, become richer, and the poor become poorer. This is the distinctive feature of Hindu society! Does it mean that we as Indians should assist in maintaining such a system?

The preservation of individualistic traits is, primarily, the philosophy of individual development. However, attaining individual development is not possible in an unequal economic system; to foster it you have to create a society without exploitation. The idea of achieving individual development is not found in Golwalkar's thoughts on the preservation of individualistic traits. That is why he does not have scientific answers to social and national questions. In several countries of the world, individual development is not possible because of adverse and hostile geographical conditions, and, so, social and political movements have emerged from modern ideologies. But Golwalkar does not give credence to such ideologies or '*isms*'. Negating democracy and communism, he says,

> According to the Western thought—from which both the concepts of Democracy and Communism took birth—the life of man for all practical purposes is limited to the physical plane. And *the human being is just a bundle of physical wants* [emphasis added]. Accordingly, production and distribution of material objects which were believed to satisfy the material appetites of man became the one all-consuming passion of all their theories.

Golwalkar's misunderstandings about democracy, communism and other modern theories based on materialism are reflected in his writings, which contain many prejudices against the philosophy of materialism. His texts provide enough to conclude that his campaign against the philosophy of materialism is deliberate and systematic. By defining a human being living in a socialist society as 'a bundle of physical wants'—whereas no Indian or Western philosopher favouring materialism has said so—Golwalkar has consciously developed an evil device to spread his ideas against materialism. In the evolution of Indian thinking, the lineage of materialist thought is an important philosophical tradition. It is important to note that the study of materialism is more developed in today's world than the study of spiritualism. Karl Marx himself did not describe human beings as 'a bundle of physical wants'; he made no such mention in his doctoral thesis.[3] But those who are engaged in producing propagandist literature are not interested in understanding the literatures of others. Golwalkar Guruji, therefore, rejected both principles—democracy and communism—without understanding them. This is why it was not possible for Golwalkar and his followers to find scientific ideas to explain individual development.

When you negate or enormously devalue science, scientific thought and the philosophy of materialism, you escape into spiritualism, and then you need to attach unnecessary significance to religion, gods, and sacred texts, etc. Golwalkar had no alternative but to fall into this trap in his discourse. His claim is very huge:

> . . . [T]he mission of reorganising the Hindu people on the lines of their unique national genius which the Sangh has taken up is not only a great process of true national regeneration of Bharat but also the inevitable precondition to realise the dream of world unity and human welfare. For, as we have seen, it is the grand world-unifying

---

[3] *The Difference between the Democritean and Epicurean Philosophy of Nature,* submitted to the University of Jena. Marx was awarded the Ph.D. in April 1841.

thought of Hindus alone that can supply the abiding basis for human brotherhood, that knowledge of the Inner Spirit which will charge the human mind with the sublime urge to toil for the happiness of mankind, while opening out full and free scope for every small life-specialty on the face of the earth to grow to its full stature. . . . This knowledge is in the custody of the Hindus alone. It is a divine trust, we may say, given to charge of the Hindus by Destiny.

According to him, this precious knowledge is contained in Rig Veda's *Purusha Sukta*:

ब्राह्मणोऽस्य मुखमासीद् बाहू राजन्यः कृतः ।
ऊरु तदस्य यद्वैश्यः पद्भ्यां शूद्रो अजायत ॥
(Brahmin is the head, King the hands, Vaishya the thighs and Shudra the feet.)

This was the ideal social structure of the Vedic period. Our ancestors have told us that our society itself is our god. By rejecting the democratic, modern socialist structure, Golwalkar embraced the ancient Chaturvarnya system of social classes. According to him, the unequal social system is the ideal that he looked forward to achieve. He says, in the course of Indian history, society distanced itself from the Rig Vedic social system and, so, social debaucheries increased. The society lost its character, and its men lost their virile powers. So he argues that if you want Indian society to be raised by powerful and virile men, you have to revitalize and protect Hindu religion.

In Hinduism's ideal social system, every *varna* must perform its pre-determined duty without being afraid of even death. *Karma* and *dharma* are integrated, and there is no distinction between them in the religion. Therefore, it is believed that, just as an individual, only when a nation sticks to its roots of *swadharma—*

Golwalkar calls it 'the duty springing from one's vocation'—does it grow and blossom into complete glory and achievement. Pulling out one's *swadharma* roots and replacing them with others will only result in total chaos and degeneration.

The basis of Golwalkar's view on sustaining individualistic traits is a static religious thought. It states that an individual must continue to work as per the sanction of religion without being afraid of death. He cites the *Bhagvad Gita*:

स्वधर्मे निधनं श्रेयः परधर्मो भयावहः ।

(Even death while performing one's own *dharma* brings blessedness; taking to another's *dharma* is fraught with fearful consequences.)

Golwalkar approves of this static view of religion. He constructs his ideas on the basis of spiritualism. But, in this approach, the idea of development is static. It is therefore necessary to examine this spiritualism and its approach.

We see that Indian society has today given up its *swadharma* patterns of behaviour. Shudras, peasants and workers have given up their hereditary occupations. They are contesting elections and have thus become Kshatriyas. Rich Brahmins have given up their priestly occupation and taken up the work of Chamars—they have opened up shoe industries and have thus become Shudras. The Bahujan communities have given up their occupations and have started working in the field of education, delivering knowledge. We have also derived inspiration from Islamic and European civilizations, which led us towards social transformation. Is the transformation good or evil? Dynamism and the transfer of cultures are unique characteristics of our age. However, Golwalkar does not accept this. He says,

The task of rekindling Hindu way of life brushing off the ashes of self-forgetfulness and imitation covering the immortal embers of the age-old *samskaras* in the Hindu heart so that pure flame of the National Self of this sacred land will once again blaze forth in all its effulgence, therefore, comes before us as the call of National *Swadharma*.

Golwalkar has declared that this Hindu perception is good for Hindustan. He reiterates that the ancient identity of our nation has not yet been entirely annihilated. He wants to build this grand ideal and the racial spirit once again. So, he hopes to revive the era of great spiritual and national heroes, and says,

> Remember that the ancient spirit is not dead. That race spirit, which has survived all the shocks of centuries of aggression and has time and again thrown up great spiritual and national heroes, is bound to reassert itself. Let us fashion our life on the pattern of those ancient torch-bearers, those cultural luminaries of our land. Let us revive that glorious tradition which produced a Vasishtha, a Vishwamitra, a Chanakya, a Vidyaranya and a Samartha, that blossomed forth in a Sri Rama, a Chandragupta, a Krishnadevaraya and a Shivaji.

He should have examined this tradition adequately and understood it. Missing from his list are Buddha, Mahavira, Charvaka, Basavanna, Tukaram, Ashoka and Akbar, among others. So, the tradition that he speaks of is the Brahminical tradition. His list of names displays the Brahminical domination of tradition, and the major function of the RSS is to revive this dominant Brahminical tradition. This is Golwalkar's thought process when he explains the nature and responsibility of the RSS.

Broadly speaking, so far we have discussed the approaches, aims and objectives of the RSS. Hedgewar, Golwalkar and Balasaheb Deoras devoted their lives to the RSS with missionary zeal. Their devotion, character and loyalty to the Sangh have attracted young people to work for the organization and take up an active role in its development. This fascination has sustained in the country's youth. Since its inception, the Sangh has been busy propagating and reviving Chaturvarnya by citing the personal traits and qualities of the Sangh's radical personalities. It never occurred to the youth that a critical inquiry is required. Guruji presented a discourse of Indian history through spiritual expression. Taking advantage of the ignorance and prejudice towards the philosophy of materialism amongst the youth and others, he perpetually dismissed democratic socialism. Nevertheless, one cannot blame him or the Sangh for such an attempt.

Progressive movements were introduced in this country around 150 years ago. However, those who invested their faith in democratic values completely failed to introduce the Indian materialist traditions to the youth. The relevant question is: why were Indian materialist traditions defamed despite being able and strong? What are the fundamental differences between spiritualism and materialism? We did not comprehensively discuss these questions, and neither were in-depth studies commissioned. Although Indian socialists and communists embraced the philosophy of materialism, there remains a good deal of confusion among them while discussing Indian history from the materialist point of view. It has been a difficult task for them. The socialists could not accomplish it successfully at length, and whatever was achieved in this context did not reach the country's youth. As a result, they are attracted to the distorted history presented by Golwalkar. Not Golwalkar, but the socialists and communists of our country should be blamed for not correctly conveying history.

In *Bunch of Thoughts*, Golwalkar presents India's history in an attractive and fascinating way. However, he does not discuss it in a scientific and objective manner. Socialism possesses an effective tool for analysing history in a scientific way, but the tool was unacceptable to Golwalkar because he did not believe in the principle of economic equality. Even though a criticism of Indian history is possible from the materialist point of view, he summarily dismissed the possibility and rejected the tools made available by materialist philosophy. The principal reason was that he saw a risk in it and he feared that the seeds of socialist materialism might be sown in Indian society. So, instead of evaluating history, he laid emphasis on historical events. He distorted history with attractive and fascinating presentations. Therefore, it is necessary to extensively examine it. The basis of the values on which Golwalkar built a framework of Indian history, and its critical examination, can lead us to the principal reasons for the rise of the RSS. Discovering the sources of this rise would make it easier for us to ponder upon the prospects for its transformation, its limitations, and what the Indian labouring class could expect from the Sangh. We could look for answers in this line of inquiry.

## 2. FRAMEWORK OF HISTORY

M.S. Golwalkar's idea of history is entirely based on an idealist approach. The clash between the discourses of spiritualism and materialism has been a major controversy all over the world, and it has an important place in the Indian philosophical tradition too. In Hindu philosophy, 'Brahman' connotes the ultimate truth and ultimate reality. It is the cosmic spirit, which has no form, is pervasive and unchanging, and which unites the universe. On the contrary, materialism believes that the presence of matter is a prerequisite for consciousness, and, thereby, for spiritual feelings or emotions. Indian materialist philosophers, the Charvakas, defined materialism as 'भूतेभ्यः चैतन्यम्', i.e. consciousness is a product of matter. Chaitanyavad, or spiritualism—which became equated with metaphysics—is a static philosophy. Chaitanyavad considers the spirit to be a mystical substance, sacred, as well as *apaurusheya* (not of human origin). After spirituality became attached with these values, the Indian *smrutikars*[1] elevated Vedanta[2] as *Dharmashastras*, or religious texts, and cultivated Chaitanyavad as an ideology. This put an end to the dynamic character of Vedanta. *Manusmruti* and Vedanta were fashioned into strong ideological weapons to propagate caste and class exploitation, which stagnated Hindu society.

[1] The followers of *Manusmruti*.
[2] Vedanta, or 'end of the Vedas', refers to the philosophical speculations on each of the four Vedas, which we know as the Upanishads. It is also used to refer to the various schools of thought that emerged in the Classical period that were based largely on the Upanishads, among other texts.

Materialism is a dynamic philosophy. It formulated the tools by which we could decipher the mysteries of the universe and its evolution. It also enabled us to understand the distinct stages of human history. However, such a critical inquiry is not possible in spiritualism because the very basis of spiritual philosophy is static. So how can it explain the dynamics of the changing world? Although Vedantists accepted spiritualism, their idealism could not interpret the changes in society. That is why the Vedantas contain multiple interpretations, several of which are also contradictory. As they are contradictory, the Vedantas cannot explain reality. No static philosophy can interpret reality, which is composed of the dynamic physical world. The Vedantists took self-opposing approaches while attempting the interpretations, but they did not accredit materialist philosophy. Therefore, interpretations of spiritualism in the *Bhagvad Gita* and devotional Bhakti poetry, and those by Chanakya, Shankaracharya, Mahatma Gandhi and Lokmanya Tilak, as well as other interpretations of Vedanta during the colonial era, are all contradictory. While singing praises of the Vedas and glorifying Hindu culture, and opposing modern ideologies, Golwalkar seems to be completely befuddled. He argues that the principle of socialism, which aims for a society free of subjugation and oppression, is irrelevant to Hindu tradition. In *Bunch of Thoughts*, he claims that Indian philosophy has pictured the highest state of society and offered a cogent explanation for it, quoting from the *Mahabharata*:

न राज्यं न च राजाऽसीत् दण्डयो न च दाण्डिक: ।
धर्मेणैव प्रजास्सर्वाः रक्षन्ति स्म परस्परम् ॥

(There existed no state, no king, no penalty and no criminals. All protected one another by virtue of *dharma*.)

*Dharma* is the universal code of right conduct that awakens the Common Inner Bond, restrains selfishness, and keeps the people together in that harmonious state even without external authority. There will be no selfishness, no hoarding and all men will live and work for the whole.

In this vision, there is no governing system nor any government; there are no criminals nor any authority to mete out punishment. The religion is itself the governing system. This stage of primitive communism is referred to in the *Mahabharata* as the supreme stage of human society, in which *dharma* and *karma* were important. Although this fanciful depiction can entertain us for some time, it does not inspire social change. While embracing the approaches from the spiritualist Vedanta, the RSS is revitalizing the Vedic Chaturvarnya system. And, if they did give up this Vedantic approach, they might come up with any number of interpretations, obviously none of which would be progressive. I think that the Sangh wants to sustain casteist domination by throwing dust into people's eyes and blinding a majority of them. Such attempts have been made several times in the country's history. Progressive democratic organizations must keep abreast of them as they happen.

The main objective of the Sangh is to revive Vedic ideology and, accordingly, produce a new social system—this was Golwalkar's unequivocal declaration. The third and current *sarsanghchalak* (chief of the Sangh), Madhukar Dattatraya 'Balasaheb' Deoras, did not modify Golwalkar's plan either. Although he said 'the Sangh is going to change', he never illustrated the details of the change. The Sangh employs this diplomatic technique, and it uses radio, television and other media to propagate its ideas.

The Rig Vedic age in Indian history was a period of primitive tribal communism; the institution of family was not yet established then. The Dasa and Dasyu[3] were killed by the Aryans, and women

[3] In the Rig Veda, Dasa and Dasyu are names given to the aboriginal tribes

and cattle were snatched away from these non-Aryan communities. So, the Rig Vedic Aryans lived luxuriously, consuming the spoils. The Sanghists, Vedists, and Hinduists reiterate stories from the Rig Veda, which is said to be *apaurusheya*, or divinely originated, to glorify a convenient history.[4]

No socialist has neglected the historical significance of religion. In India, from Dr. Ram Manohar Lohia to Jayaprakash Narayan, and, internationally, Karl Marx to Mao Tse-tung—each of them was aware of it. Lohia built a movement to destroy *varna* and caste systems in India. Jayaprakash started a campaign denouncing the Brahmin sacred thread (*janeu*). Dr. B.R. Ambedkar proved, in his innumerable documents, that Hindu civilization was 'infamy'. Marx and Mao considered religion to be a means of exploitation. It is true that human beings achieve solace and satisfaction through religious faith. A human being who suffocates because of subjugation, and is unable to tolerate it, embraces illusions for personal consolation. However, it is pertinent to ask if one should give up such illusions. To achieve true happiness, we must give up false consolation. Subsequently, one realizes that the situations causing such illusions must be ended once and for all. This is the socialists' argument. Is the RSS ready for such a proposal?

Religion played a major role in social transformation, and it contributed to society at a time when government institutions did not exist. However, the manifestation of a superman was projected onto people. Those in power exploited the masses and lived in wealth and luxury. In the Indian tradition, a king used to

---

that fought the Indo-Aryans. The terms went on to connote 'enemy', 'servant', 'labourer' and 'dark-skinned', among other meanings.

[4] It would be interesting to read P.R. Deshmukh's book entitled *Indus Civilisation, Rigveda and Hindu Culture* (Nagpur: Saroj Prakashan, 1982). Deshmukh has made tremendous efforts in throwing light on complex issues and offers an assessment of how the Aryans established domination over non-Aryans.

salute a *rushi* (sage), who gave up all worldly happiness. Golwalkar admires this tradition with an air of pride. But was a king prepared to renounce his entire wealth that was accumulated through plunder? Is the Hindu culture superior only because kings saluted the *rushis* who renounced everything? And if the *rushis* fighting to acquire knowledge were beheaded by kings, what kind of culture did such kings produce? Do Golwalkar's followers mean to suggest that such kings were not found in Hindu culture? But they don't address such questions. Religious powers, priests and politicians created a class that subjugated the common people. Hindu religion is not an exception to this. In the course of history, several clashes have taken place between groups that exploited others. The Upanishads, like *Katha, Kena, Chandogya, Bruhadaranyaka* and *Mundaka*, bear witness to the confrontations between Brahmins and Kshatriyas that occurred during the time the texts were composed. In the period after Buddha and Mahavira, the *Bhagvad Gita* was employed to resolve problems, and *Manusmruti* succeeded in establishing the hegemony of Brahmins once again. The principal concern for Hinduists in the modern period has been to maintain the dominance of Hindu culture through *Manusmruti* and the *Gita*. To do this, they required a platform from where they could sing paeans about the bravery and heroic deeds of historical figures. The problem was solved by establishing the RSS in 1925. The birth of RSS was, thus, a result of the need to provide the religious and cultural basis for exploitation of non-Brahmin people.

The genesis of the RSS must be understood in relation to the times in which it emerged. A well-organized freedom movement was proceeding under the leadership of Mohandas Karamchand Gandhi when the Sangh came into existence. Why then did the Hinduists need to establish the Sangh in 1925? The varied roles that the Sangh took on and the discreet methods that it followed from time to time must be considered to answer this question. Not every Hinduist was necessarily a supporter of the Sangh, of course.

Colonial exploitation adversely affected various classes of people in British India. The Brahmin class ruled the centres of power that were ignored by the British. The Brahmins were increasingly worried about holding on to the power centres after Independence too, and struggled to retain them. It was natural for them to have ambitions of grabbing political power when Independence came. To succeed at the task, it was necessary to gather the existing feudal kings, landlords and newly emerging capitalists of pre-Independence India. The Hinduists succeeded in mobilizing the feudal classes and neo-capitalists. But Mahatma Gandhi's movement was the biggest barrier in their path. In fact, the Indian freedom movement itself was a problem for the Sangh because of the laws for social reform enacted by the British in response to the strong social movements in the years between 1885 and 1920. The laws—which included the Indian Councils Act of 1909 (known as Morley–Minto Reforms), and the Government of India Act, 1919 (called the Montagu–Chelmsford Reforms)—opened up the possibility of parliamentary democracy getting established in India. It was becoming clear in the 1920s that more reforms would pave the way for the Indian Constitution to be drafted along the principles of parliamentary democracy. Seeking power through parliamentary elections would then not be possible for the Sangh. The political awakening in Bahujan society, or the Indian masses, was another important concern for them. The reasons for Golwalkar's strong opposition to democratic socialism are found here.

The Government of India Act of 1919 and the death of Lokmanya Balgangadhar Tilak in 1920 made the Hinduists desperate and reckless. The 1919 law gave a boost to the nurturing of democratic spirit among Indian masses, while Tilak's death loosened the grip of Brahmins over the Indian National Congress. Under the leadership of Gandhi, the non-cooperation movement, which began in 1920, energized the Indian public and produced political aspirations in them. But Gandhi created difficulties for the Hinduists by persuading Muslims and 'Untouchables' [henceforth called Dalits] to participate in the freedom movement. He supported the Khilafat movement and took an enormous interest in the problems of Dalits. The Hinduists were convinced that his moderate policy would promulgate democracy across the country, down to the root, and reach the Indian masses. Therefore, they were confronted with this great problem—Gandhi—the obstacle to their political ambitions. It was clear to them that the Congress-led struggle and moderate British policies would lead to the freedom of Indians. That was not of any advantage to Bharat Mata, the holy motherland, and so, to them, the demand for freedom was cowardice. To them, subscribing to Gandhi's tools of non-violence and *satyagraha* was a sign of weakness and of docile leadership. The Hinduists went to the extreme and promoted the idea that Gandhi was an enemy of Hindu communities. They spread such evil notions about him to produce unrest in the country.

To accomplish their mission, the Hinduists formed the RSS and forged a group of extremist youths. The group started using the language of violence—their outcry found expression in rhetoric like: 'Who's achieved freedom without spilling blood?' They proposed to fight the British by seeking help from fascist organizations in countries like Germany, Italy and Japan. Adolf Hitler was their hero. In a swirling world, where democracy was pitted against fascism, the Sangh stood with the fascists. Even today we commit the blunder of thinking that the Sangh was born to spread hatred and contempt against Muslims among the Hindus—which it did by highlighting how Gandhi was creating space for the Muslims and making allowances for them. However, the Sangh's main agenda was not hatred against Muslims, but to seek power through fascist ideology. One should never forget this. Under the leadership of Gandhi, the Congress did not allow the Sangh to spread its extremism across the country. The Sangh thus lost the possibility and hope of gaining power at the centre. However, it succeeded in generating a fascist sensibility among the youth, which resulted in the assassination of Gandhi and removed a barrier from their path. But they could not succeed in destroying the ideology of democracy, and its core values such as freedom, equality and fraternity, which were sown by him. Those who spoke the language of 'blood for freedom' spilled the blood of Gandhi, but they did not feel it necessary to spill the blood of the British.

The RSS chief, Balasaheb Deoras, has said that the organization would remain alienated from politics. The meaning of this statement must be carefully understood. Does the Sangh not want power by contesting elections as a political party? Even if the RSS became a political party, would it come to power through elections? The Sangh knows it only too well that it will not gain authority that way. Therefore, instead of playing the role of a political party, the Sangh wants to be a political pressure group in national politics. A pressure group takes advantage of opportunities and influences political parties. It can even compel a government to take decisions that suit its selfish ends. Every pressure group engages in coercive actions. The Sangh too follows the same policy. It often gets confusing when the Sangh begins to engage with its opposition—it becomes political when it wants to, while conveniently claiming to be non-political in other instances.

It is because of such a dichotomy and its serpentine aims and objectives that the RSS will never alter its core character. If the Sangh decides to change itself, it won't have an independent existence in national politics. If interviews of Deoras are read carefully, it is clear that he has not brought about any radical changes in the role and policies of the Sangh. Instead, he points outwards and says people's prejudices towards the Sangh have not diminished. Progressive forces must remember that the Sangh will not change so easily. It will not admit Muslims in its organization and, if it did, it would be on the condition that they embrace Hinduism. Let alone the inclusion of Muslims in the Sangh, even Hindus from Bahujan and depressed communities would never be able to reach the Sangh. This is mainly because it is very difficult for the Sangh to create the space for expansion.

When the Janata government emerged [in 1977], progressive forces became worried that the Sangh might spread its network. But it is not possible for the Sangh to expand—and neither does it want to. The Sangh wants to preserve its limited but organized power. A pressure group performs a key role for the organized exploitation of the depressed and Bahujan communities, and in sustaining hegemony. It keeps alive exploitation to maintain the domination of upper castes. This is the chief purpose of a pressure group like the Sangh, which wants to sustain its dominance through exploitation.

The progressive forces of this country that are involved in the movement to achieve a society free of exploitation—for which they have to organize a class struggle—need to clearly understand the Sangh's political strategies. As long as hegemony remains the purpose of the upper castes and classes, the Sangh's existence is inevitable. Their ideology and uncompromising mentality will remain the same, even though it manifests in different forms.

Fundamental differences will always exist in the philosophical, social, political, and economic thinking of the progressive, democratic and socialistic forces, and the Sangh. It is hoped that the many compromises made by the Janata government with the Bharatiya Jan Sangh do not lead to chaos. However, it must be understood that compromising with the Bharatiya Jan Sangh on democratic socialism will be self-destructive. Opposition groups came together and formed the Janata Party in response to Indira Gandhi's fascist mentality, while it was the Sangh's fascist mentality that facilitated the disintegration of the Janata Party. This is why progressive forces must get together to fight and confront the Sangh on every issue.

## 3. HINDUISM AS NATIONALISM

It has been repeatedly claimed by the Rashtriya Swayamsevak Sangh that it is a 'nationalist organization' which has played an important role in the nation's history. In this context, to comprehensively understand the nationalism of the Sangh we must raise and discuss questions such as what is a nation and what are the major limitations of nationalism.

Golwalkar refuses the concept of 'nation' established in the West, and goes on to define the nation in his own way:

> . . . [P]eople should not be just a mass of men, just a juxtaposition of heterogeneous individuals. They should have evolved a definite way of life moulded by community of life ideals, of culture, of feelings, sentiments, faith, and traditions. If people thus become united in a coherent and well-organised society having common traditions and aspirations, a common memory of the happy and unhappy experience of their past life, common feelings of friendship and hostility, and their interests intertwined in one identical whole— then such people living as children of that particular territory may be termed as a 'nation'.

Is India a nation? We shall arrive at the answer to this key question a little later. But before that we must examine, first of all, with the help of Golwalkar's *Bunch of Thoughts*, in what sense does Golwalkar identify India as a nation, and in what way does he apply the concept of nationalism to India. According to him, from the

Himalayan region in the north, Iran to the west, Singapore to the east and Sri Lanka to the south—the integrated region bounded by the ocean on three sides and the mountains at the top is where a society was developed by the people who have recently been identified as Hindus. The ancestors of these Hindus developed the ideals of love and devotion towards the region and the land and it is they who produced its traditions. Golwalkar has described this territory as the motherland. Sacred duties and religious rites were prescribed by Hindu ancestors with the purpose of producing the sentiment that this land is godly. Golwalkar argues that the people inhabiting the land from Kashi [Varanasi] to Kanyakumari, tribal to urban, are all connected by blood and devotional ties. He cites the Vedas to support this argument:

माता भूमिः पुत्रोऽहम् पृथिव्याः ।
(This earth is my mother and I am her son.)

उत्तरं यत्समुद्रस्य हिमाद्रेश्चैव दक्षिणम् ।
वर्षं तद् भारतं नाम भारती यत्र संततिः ॥
(The land to the north of the oceans and the south of the Himalaya is called Bharatvarsha, and Bharatis are her children.)

He cites Chanakya's description:

हिमवत्समुद्रान्तरमुदीचीनं योजनसहस्त्रपरिमाणम् ।
(To the north of the oceans to the Himalaya, the country is 1,000 *yojanas* in length.)

Golwalkar also reproduces a verse dedicated to the rivers that are held sacred and says they too are '. . . a lesson in devotion, because we are made to feel that even a drop of water from these holy rivers [has] the potency of wiping out all our sins':

गङ्गे च यमुने चैव गोदावरि सरस्वति ।
नर्मदे सिन्धु कावेरि जलेऽस्मिन् सन्निधिं कुरु ॥

(In this water, I invoke the presence of holy waters from the rivers Ganga, Yamuna, Godavari, Saraswati, Narmada, Sindhu and Kaveri.)

This is how emotional appeals are made about the land. He records the Hindu custom of stepping out of bed and seeking Mother Earth's forgiveness for touching her with his feet:

समुद्रवसने देवि पर्वतस्तनमण्डले ।
विष्णुपत्नि नमस्तुभ्यं पादस्पर्शं क्षमस्वमे ॥

(O mother, the Divine Consort of Almighty with ocean as Thy embroidery and mountains as Thy breasts, forgive me for touching thee with my feet.)

The lyrical and poetic depictions of our country in ancient Sanskrit literature are captivating. Excerpts from a variety of sources such as those above have been cited by Golwalkar to glorify the motherland.

After the geographical scope of the land, Golwalkar turns to *bhakti* (devotion) as an important element in supporting the nation. To ascribe the status of motherland to the geographical entity, Golwalkar has no option other than to cultivate the idea of *bhakti*, because he refuses to accept the philosophy of materialism.

How can one activate sentiments for the motherland without *bhakti*? Golwalkar addresses this question to Indians. Terming the formal methods of worship in religious devotion as passive, he argues for a 'dynamic' kind of devotion to be kept alive among Indians:

The dynamic aspect of devotion is to manifest in practical national life a spirit of readiness to sacrifice our all for the protection of the freedom and honour of every speck of this motherland. It is this active manifestation that counts in this hard matter-of-fact world. A heart fired with such devotion can never tolerate the slightest affront to the object of its devotion, i.e., the motherland. . . . A divine discontent to undo all the past insults and humiliations burns in such a heart.

He attributes Partition to a lack of devotion to the motherland among India's leaders. Blaming the leaders and others for celebrating Independence, he expresses his frustration with rhetorical questions:

Is this fiery and heroic aspect of devotion to our motherland alive in our hearts today? If that spirit had been there in our leaders and in our common folk, could Partition have taken place? Would they not have risen uncompromisingly, heroically as one man against all such machinations of the British and the Muslim, prepared to shed their last drop of blood for maintaining the scared integrity of the motherland? Alas, that did not happen. On the contrary, people, led by the leaders, were busy in celebrations on the advent of so-called independence!

After region and devotion, Golwalkar considers religion to be of extraordinary importance for nationalism. He proclaims Hinduism as supreme among all religions in the world. According to him, the Chaturvarnya system described in the Rig Veda represents the four-dimensional form of the supreme god:

Society was conceived of as the fourfold manifestation of the Almighty to be worshipped by all, each in his own way and according to his capacity. If a Brahaman became great by imparting knowledge, a Kshatriya was hailed equally great for destroying the enemy. No less important was the Vaishya who fed and sustained society through agriculture and trade or the Shudra who served society through his art and craft. Together and by their mutual interdependence in a spirit of identity, they constituted the social order.

He defends the Chaturvarnya system despite agreeing that it has created inequality:

The felling [sic] of inequality, of high and low, which has crept into the *Varna* system, is comparatively of recent origin. . . . But in its original form, the distinctions in that social order did not imply any discrimination such as big and small, high and low, among its constituents. . . .

Calling the caste system the 'highest evolved state of society', Golwalkar presents an interesting interpretation of the idea of caste annihilation:

The present-day mind (accustomed to viewing things through the medium of foreign '-isms') with their high-sounding slogans of 'equality', has failed to grasp this unique feature ['highest evolved state of society'] and has raised the cry that the various diversities of our life are all so many sources of dissension and should therefore be eradicated and rolled into 'classless' society. Merely because the various limbs and organs in a body appear different and play their own specific functions, should we call them different 'classes' and proceed to remove them all to make the body a 'classless entity'? If we do that, will that be evolution or murder?

Golwalkar refers to the caste system in Indian society as a blessing. He argues that it was the caste system that prevented our country from going into the hands of foreign rulers in ancient times. To explicate his argument, he suggests an eccentric idea:

> Even during the past one thousand years when our nation fell before foreign onslaughts, there is no instance on record to show that caste distinctions were at the root of our national disunity that helped the invaders to conquer us.
>
> If the caste system had really been the root cause of our weakness, then our people should have succumbed to foreign invasions far more easily than those people who had no castes.

Golwalkar illustrates the idea with such examples from the past:

> The person responsible for the defeat of Prithviraj, the Hindu King at Delhi, by Mohammed Ghori was his own caste-relation Jayachand. The person who hounded Rana Pratap from forest to forest was none other than his own caste-man Raja Mansingh. Shivaji too was opposed by men of his own caste. Even in the last-ditch battle between the Hindus and the British at Poona in 1818, it was a fellow caste-man of the Peshawas, Natu by name, who lowered the Hindu flag and hoisted the British flag. There was a veritable race of such traitors but they were so because they fell a prey to other temptations and for other reasons. Caste never came into [the] picture.

Narrating such slices of history, Golwalkar blames a community of 'traitors' who existed during those periods. He brands them as a race, and claims that they did not have any relationship with the institution of caste. A casteless society, he adds, would have been more easily victimized by foreign invaders. Thus, Golwalkar infers, the caste system prevented India from falling victim to foreign invasions. While exploring these events, he goes on to explain history:

We know as a matter of history that our northwestern and northeastern areas, where the influence of Buddhism had disrupted the caste system, fell an easy prey to the onslaughts of Muslims. Gandhar, now called Kandahar, became completely Muslimised. Conversion took a heavy toll in East Bengal also. But the areas of Delhi and Uttar Pradesh, which were considered to be very orthodox and rigid in caste restrictions, remained predominantly Hindu even after remaining as the citadels of Muslim power and fanaticism for a number of centuries. We know that even as late as Shivaji's times, the so-called 'low-caste' also played an epic role in the resurrection of *swaraj*.

Golwalkar equates Hinduism with Indian nationalism. Therefore, he defines nationalism as Hinduism.

The RSS is a very different kind of an organization than the many social and political groups that have worked in the nation during the last century. It has been noticed since the time the Sangh was established, people connected with it have a different attitude. Their nationalistic fervour is peculiar and extreme when compared to other nationalist organizations. This unique difference is noticed in the day-to-day actions and behaviour of the Sangh's people—especially when they fervently criticize the Left organizations and label materialist philosophy as anti-nationalist. They assert that only their nationalistic fervour is genuine and it is the only nationalism that can exist. This egotistical approach, which assumes the highest sense of superiority, manifests in the actions of the Sangh. For the Sangh, Hinduism is itself the index of nationalism.

According to Golwalkar, every particle of the geographical region of India, even dust, contains godliness, and so the land is holy to us. He says,

Nothing can be holier to us than this holy land. Every particle of dust, everything living or non-living, every stock and stone, tree and rivulet of this land is holy to us. To keep this intense devotion ever alive in the heart of every child of this soil, so many procedures and conventions were established here in the past. . . .

It is interesting how Golwalkar perceives an Indian. While reading his book, one finds that natural phenomena such as mountains, peaks, trees and oceans are reference points for defining the concept of nationalism. But what about the human beings?

A nation is meant for people—it is a space for people to enrich their lives. Nationalism can be understood as the expression of people's psychological integration. In other words, peoples' thinking, their suffering, their attitudes, etc., can be traced in the composition of a nation. Are we going to forget people while defining the nation? What about those people whose psychological integration is necessary for the composition of the nation? What place does Hinduism have for them? What is it going to do for them? Golwalkar does not wish to think of these people while defining his idea of Hindu nationalism. In fact, Hinduists would never be able to think about this because they believe that Shankaracharya's philosophy, '*Nitya-anitya-vastu-viveka*' (the intellect that discriminates between the reality and illusion of things), is the ideological basis of Hinduism. Golwalkar uses it to emphasize the notion that the country is permanent and hence greater than people. He explains that the goal of philosophy is to attain *param vaibhavam*, i.e. national glory, and he extends that concept to define nationalism. Although an individual needs institutions such as society, nation and religion, where his pleasures, miseries, wrath, greed, love, hatred, valour, cowardice, passion and lust may find expression, Golwalkar regards these emotions as worthless and trivial. He considers them as low and of baser grade. In his opinion, the only admirable emotion is devotion because only *bhakti* has a higher place; the remaining emotions must be discarded by individuals. He says,

> There is one more way of looking at this blending of the development of the individual with the integrity and welfare of society. We have been told by our great thought-givers to discriminate between what is permanent and what is impermanent. Shankaracharya has called it *nityanitya-vastu-viveka*. Let's us, for the time being, keep apart its high philosophical interpretations and apply it to our national life. Individuals come and go. Countless generations have come and gone. But the nation has remained [...] The 'permanent', therefore, is the national life. The 'impermanent' is the individual. The ideal arrangement would therefore be to transform the impermanent— the individual—into a means to attain the permanent—the social good—which would at the same time enable the individual to enrich and bring to blossom his latent divinity.

The Hinduists have accepted Shankaracharya's theoretical insights in the relationship between means and ends. The relationship that democratic socialists consider between means and ends is extraordinarily contrary to Golwalkar's understanding. What are the ends? What are the tools? Does the nation exist for individuals or do individuals exist for the nation? Is the nation a means and individuals its end? Does society stand for enrichment and excellence of individuals, or an individual for society's? The distinction between the two polarities is fundamental and it will remain pertinent for all time.

For over a hundred years, democratic socialist movements in India have given importance to the individual and advocated the fourfold principle of democracy, which says that individuals are ends in themselves; the rights enjoyed by an individual cannot be transferred or given away; an individual should not rule over others; and the rights acquired in our practical life must not be relinquished. Whereas Hinduism considers an individual only as a means, democratic socialism vehemently opposes that principle. Therefore, Golwalkar is against the ideology of democracy. He does not reject the principles of democracy simply because they are based on the philosophy of materialism, but because democratic thought centres round the individual and individualism.

The Sangh has been propagating the idea that the democratic socialist movements are anti-national. For several years, the Sangh has said that it is the only nationalist group. This sentimental view is used to influence thousands of youths simply to dismantle Left movements. Therefore, it is necessary to critically examine the concept of nationalism. How are the democratic socialists, who believe that the individual is a concrete form that is not illusory, is an end and not the means, anti-national? And, how are Sanghists and the entire Hinduist camp, who consider the nation (which is an abstraction) as the end and individuals as its means, nationalists? A thorough discussion must be held in this context. It will enable us to understand the false, distorted and quaint ideas of the Sangh. Equally, it will throw light on the propensity of the Sangh to appropriate the role of nationalists.

Modern political science believes that the creation of nationality is a pre-condition for the formation of a nation. At the same time, it also explains that it is possible for a single nation to host several nationalities. Indian society includes several languages, varied customs, different religions, innumerable castes, contradictory ideologies and their unique histories. Is such a society, which is a confluence of varied and unique attributes, qualified to be called a nationality? This is an important question. We have several *-isms* and variance based on languages, regions, religions, castes, etc. So, it can be argued that whatever number of -*isms* or variations there are, those many nationalities can coexist. In a nation where the society is an amalgamation of several castes and creeds, nationalist ideology is decided by the dominant nationality. If there are two races in a nation, the dominant race would become the nation. The caste or the language that acquires power and economic strength will become the nation. The rest are expected to live under that umbrella; the meeker nationalities serving and worshipping the stronger nationality. What did Hitler do with Jews in Germany? And what did Muslims do with Hindus in Pakistan? This history is recent and fresh.

What is the kind of nationalism in the Sangh's scheme? One can clearly understand it by their motto: Hinduism is nationalism. A majority of the people in our nation are Hindus and many of them are living miserable lives, below the poverty line. What does the Sangh's nationalism mean to the poor people? To answer the question, we have to return to Indian history again and again. In reality, the term 'Hindu' has been applied to the Indian community very recently. It was a term used by the Persian invaders. The people who were located on the banks of River Indus, also known as Sindhu, were referred to as 'Sindhu'. But the consonant 's' was pronounced 'h' by the Persians, and so we were called Hindu instead of Sindhu. These interpretations are made by historiographers. Golwalkar says that it is not historically correct to claim that the term Hindu is of recent origin, or that foreigners designated it. 'Hindu' is essentially regional, he says:

> We find the name *Sapta-sindhu* in the oldest records of the world—the Rig Veda itself—as an epithet applied to our land and our people. And it is also well known that the syllable 'S' in Sanskrit is at times changed to 'H' as [in] some of our Prakrit languages and even in European languages. And thus the name *Hapta-Hindu* and then

*Hindu* came into currency. Thus *Hindu* is a proud name of our own origin and others learnt to denote us by it only later on.

Golwalkar rightly observes that the term 'Bharatiya' is a substitute for 'Hindu' and the Vedas also validate this claim. In the Rig Veda, we are described as 'Sapta-sindhu' but not Hindu. The name 'Hindu' was used to address us Indians, or the Bharatiya people, by foreign invaders. In spite of his agreement with the origin of the nomenclature, why does Golwalkar insist on using the term 'Hindu'? His argument is quite interesting:

> *Bharatiya* too is an ancient name associated with us since hoary times. The name Bharat appears even in the Vedas. Our Puranas have also spoken of our motherland as Bharat and of our people as *Bharatis* in fact [*sic*], it connotes the same meaning as 'Hindu'. But today, there is misconception regarding the word *Bharatiya* also. It is commonly used as a translation of the word 'Indian', which includes all the various other communities like the Muslim, Christian, Parsi, etc., residing in this land. So, the word *'Bharatiya'* too is likely to mislead us when we want to denote our particular society. The word 'Hindu' alone connotes correctly and completely the meaning which we want to convey.

What then is the correct and complete interpretation of the term 'Hindu'? Connotations of the term used by Golwalkar must be examined carefully.

New studies on Indus Valley Civilization have been emerging in recent times. The insights from excavations of Mohenjo-daro and Harappa have challenged the orthodox interpretations of the Vedas. The different phases of our civilization's evolution since the Vedic era have also come to light. Besides, a reinterpretation of the scriptures, mythological tales, and the Puranas, etc., has revealed the evolution of culture. Many thinkers and scholars are presenting new ideas about the evolutionary complexities of Indian historical life, and how varied communities confronted challenges and fought against their problems. So, these historical details are all now available. However, those who are unaware of history and their civilization and culture develop fake ideas about their ancestors and the past. Hegemony is developed through such falsity. It takes the form of self-pride, essentially leading to egotism and ethnocentrism.

In 1906, the Muslims of this country founded a political organization, the Muslim League, to acquire power. The organization distorted Islamic history and promoted dogmatism. The Hinduists came into politics as a response to the Muslim League. They too distorted history like the Muslim League did. This was not happening in our country alone—it was the case almost everywhere in the world where progressive movements were challenging the hegemony of a particular class. To maintain their dominance, the priestly class spread the poison of cultural hegemony. History was distorted for this sole purpose.

The rise of religion signifies an important evolutionary phase in world history. But not enough attention has been paid to this phenomenon. It is true that due to the dogmatic approach of religions, scholars neglected critical analyses of religious beliefs, scriptures, art, mythologies and historical texts. As a result, a particular class or caste maintained its command on religion. This domination of religion has a unique place in Indian history, which is comparatively more complex and intricate than histories of the rest of the world.

Hinduists neglected Indian history enormously. They did not pay enough critical attention to the evolutionary phases of the Indian people. Therefore, as compared to histories of other countries, Indian history began to look ridiculous and fuzzy. The

RSS and other Hinduist organizations have been solely responsible for the distortion of Indian history. They have taken it to a ludicrous pitch. From the point of view of Hinduist organizations, Bharatiya, i.e. Indian civilization, is confined to the Hindu civilization. This has led to twisted descriptions of historical scenarios. The RSS and other Hinduist organizations have been busy misreporting and falsifying our country's history. They have continuously created many prejudices among people through distorted historical facts, and promoted this distorted history in the nation's politics.

The Rig Veda contains descriptive accounts of the Aryans— about their origins and how they defeated pre-Aryan cultures. We find in its pages that the Dasa, Dasyu and Pani, who were enemies of the Aryans, were more civilized than the Aryans. In his writings, Prof. D.D. Kosambi attempted to explore the truths of the past reflected in these scriptures. P.R. Deshmukh wrote an important book entitled *Indus Civilisation, Rigveda and Hindu Culture*, highlighting the excavation of Mohenjo-daro and Harappa. Dr. Sumant K. Muranjan's *Purohitvargavarchasva va Bharatacha Samajik Itihas* ('Hegemony of the Priestly Class and Social History of India', 1973) provides us with analytical principles of historiography. However, when one is obsessed with the primitive notion of caste supremacy they cannot realize the value of such works. But the young generation that wants to transform this country into 'one nation' must study these books, or else their nationalism might also turn into casteism like that of the Sangh.

The Aryans were a savage community. They were foreign invaders. By contrast, the natives of this country were gentle and civilized. The history of these two groups is a history of confrontation. It is also, simultaneously, a history of cooperation. The confrontation and camaraderie between the two groups led to inter-group marriages and also an exchange of ideologies. The groups adopted each other's gods and goddesses, and religious rites. The interaction and inter-mixing between the two groups led to an amalgamation, creating a composite culture that is known as Bharatiya (Indian) culture. Vedic religion developed from those historical connections. The advent of the Vedic period brought an end to primitive culture. It was during this period that the worship of nature diminished, a graded society emerged, and *das pratha*, the system of slavery, was established. Nature deities became gods like Agni (fire), Varuna (the sky) and Usha (dawn), which were accessible to everyone. This was a time before the nation-state was formed. Religion regulated the society.

Golwalkar expresses great admiration for that state of life, but he denies that the period was primitive, or a phase when human beings still lived like savages. It was a pre-state, pre-nation and pre-government era of mankind. It was the Vedic era and not the era of the Hindus, and it was Vedic religion, not Hindu religion. The era of Hindu religion arrived innumerable years after the end of the Vedic period, by when society was fully stratified. The phase of primitive communism had ended with the Vedic era. It was at this point in time that one class began imposing its supremacy over other classes. The Brahmin class gave birth to Hindu religion to uphold its authority. This era is reflected in Chanakya's *Arthashastra*, and also in *Manusmruti* and other *smrutis*. The Vedic religion was altered and narrowed down. The inclusive gods and goddesses of the early-Vedic classless society became exclusive in the Hindu religion. They were walled off in temple precincts, which were the domain of only specific people who were allowed to enter and worship. In the name of religion, vast amounts of funds were accumulated through *dakshina* (donations). The priests amassed huge shares of wealth through deception and intellectual arrogance, and with that they garnered political power. Brahmin authority was thus initiated in the name of Hindu religion. Brahmin power remains active without any hindrance even today—the Brahmins do not want to change this well-established system. They are desperate to safeguard the Brahminical upper hand in every way. In fact, the modern Hinduist organizations are an incarnation of the erstwhile Brahminical power. It is the communal root of the RSS.

This clarifies why Golwalkar insisted on using the term 'Hindu' instead of 'Bharatiya'. 'Bharatiya' is connected to Vedic culture and the period when the state as an institution did not exist. The term 'Bharatiya' is more inclusive and does not signify Brahminical supremacy. The term 'Hindu' is fundamentally linked to the Brahminical cult and its supremacy. 'Hindu' offers an expedient method for the Brahmin class to control political power. It is therefore difficult for Golwalkar and Hinduist organizations to be associated with 'Bharatiya'. Instead, for Golwalkar, 'Hindu' denotes Indian society. So, one should have no problem in understanding why Golwalkar assigns the term 'Hindu'.

In this context, it is necessary to discuss the 11th and 12th couplets of *Purusha Sukta* in Rig Veda, which mention the Chaturvarnya system. It is not possible that these couplets were composed in the Vedic period. One can be confident that they were inserted into the Rig Veda only after Brahmins created favourable conditions for their dominion to grow in Indian society. These couplets have no relation to the verses that precede and succeed them in the *Purusha Sukta*. Some scholars believe that the couplets were imposed on the Vedic text. However, till date, a satisfactory critical enquiry has not been attempted.

The RSS and other Hinduist organizations use the term Hindu in place of Bharatiya while discussing Indian nationalism—they define Hinduism as nationalism. This is why the RSS and the entire camp of Hinduist organizations take an extreme position, and they call all non-Hindus 'anti-nationals' and 'traitors'. It is important to know why these organizations take this fanatical stance. Likewise, it is also important to examine the phenomenon and separate fact from fiction. In his book, Golwalkar has discussed in detail the nature of the Hindu system. Lala Hardayal, the well-known revolutionary, had once told Golwalkar a story to explain the kind of Hindu society that ought to exist in the country. Golwalkar cites it in *Bunch of Thoughts*. It is worth quoting it here because it illustrates the kind of society that Hinduists wish for:

> There is an incident narrated by Lala Hardayal, one of our great revolutionaries. In the south, there was an English officer. His assistant was a local person, probably a Naidu. The orderly of that Englishman was a Brahmin. One day, when the Englishman was walking in a street, followed by his orderly, the assistant came from the opposite side. The two officers greeted each other and shook hands. But when the assistant officer saw the orderly, he took off his turban and touched his feet. The Englishman was amazed. He queried, 'I am your senior officer, but you stand erect and just shake hands with me, whereas he is only my peon and you prostrate before him on this busy road. What is the matter?' The assistant officer explained, 'You may be my officer, but you are a mlechha. He may be a peon, but he belongs to the class of my people which is held in great respect all down the centuries, before whom it is my duty to bow down.'

The story cited by Golwalkar portrays the ideal Hindu social system and projects the social structure that the Hinduists want to nurture in reality. It also depicts the desirable mutual relationship between Hindu Brahmins and non-Brahmin communities. It highlights the mindset required by the ideal Hindu social system. The RSS wants to produce such a social system, and, obviously, the democratic socialists will fervently oppose it even at the cost of their lives. Therefore, a clash between the two is unavoidable even today. Golwalkar believes that the colonial British rulers had sought to corrupt the Brahmins in order to reduce the status and position they occupied in society. This is not fully true. In reality, the priestly class promoted Hindu religion over the Vedic religion. Brahmin power was established by imposing inhuman and evil customs and traditions on Bahujan communities in the name of religion. Since then, Brahmins degenerated and have been demoralized in the real sense. The seeds of their self-destruction were sown when they started to foist their control over other communities. Who is responsible for this? The priestly class pushed millions of Indians into darkness and ignorance. Indian history is filled with hard evidence of this evil conspiracy of Brahminical politics. Brahmins also succeeded in keeping a close eye on the ruling class, i.e. Kshatriyas, and controlled power at their convenience. To achieve control, they took advantage of the ignorance and religious sentiments of millions of Indian Dalit and Bahujan communities. This cultural politics helped them crush the mutinous movements arising against them. It is indeed an astounding chapter in world history—by protecting their vested interests and solidifying their hold on the other castes, Brahmins destroyed an entire nation.

The idea of affixing caste at birth was introduced by the Brahmins. Even so, the entire Brahmin camp is not involved in the politics of hegemony. Just as there are leaders, thinkers and creative writers in Brahmin society who fight for Brahminical domination, there are innumerable Brahmins who have thwarted Brahmin supremacy. Moreover, many have fought for equality and social and economic justice for the country's common people. Although traditional Brahmins by birth, they have led reformist movements at times. There are also many Brahmins who objected to the dominance of any caste over another. However, the Brahmins who worked in favour of the common people were ridiculed by Hinduists! Leaders like Gopal Ganesh Agarkar, Comrade Shripad Amrut Dange and S.M. Joshi suffered severe criticism. So, a distinction has to be made between Brahmins who maintained their caste's domination and those who refuted hegemony. Also, we find many non-Brahmins, who for their selfish ends align with the Brahmins, and many who campaign for equality and social and economic justice alongside progressive Brahmins. We must always remember this contrast in our discourse on hegemony.

Politics in India has become terribly complex and perplexing. The leaders who are Brahmin by caste are dumped into a single category. This is a poisonous tendency consciously sown in our national politics. The strategy is designed to attack casteism with casteism. In Maharashtra, such moves are clearly seen in the highest levels of politics. Casteism cannot be eliminated by practising casteism. On the contrary, such an attempt leads to a new form of casteism, a new mob rule and new fascist consciousness. This casteism, whether in the name of the Brahmin or Maratha, Dalit or Jat, Nambudiri or Naidu, is the same. They are all birds of the same feather. None of them is a true nationalist or a lover of the nation. Each one of them is selfish and entirely casteist. Their mentality is to protect the vested interests of the rich class or of a particular ruling caste.

Golwalkar falsifies history and deceptively gives a favourable basis for the Chaturvarnya system—through which he seeks to incite pride in the caste system. It is simply rhetoric. He mainly argues that the caste system came into existence during ancient times and that it did not destroy anything. On the contrary, the caste system was an advantage in the course of history, he says. Stating that today's caste system is degraded, he argues that it is so because it does not follow the original *varna* system.[1] However, he does not command his *swayamsevaks*, the volunteers, to end

---

[1] Golwalkar tries to differentiate between *varna* (class) and *jati* (caste) by saying that *varna* is good and *jati* is bad. But he ignores the fact that *varna* is the mother of caste.

the caste system—because, to him, a casteless society is absurd and inconceivable. Although Golwalkar agrees that the caste system is corrupt, he invents history to justify caste. It is not a true interpretation of history because Golwalkar does not attempt to evaluate history. Instead, he manipulates history to perpetuate Brahminical hegemony.

Millions of people from Bahujan and Dalit communities have been pushed into a world of ignorance and poverty. One of the main reasons for this is that the theory of Chaturvarnya has been interpreted by Brahmins as per their convenience. Moreover, to sustain their selfish goals, they added even more convenient interpretations and exploited the Bahujan communities as much as possible. This is the principal cause of the deterioration of this country. It is also the main barrier for progressive people who walk on the path of social and economic justice for people's welfare. This was evident when Mahatma Gandhi was assassinated. Several historians and thinkers argue on similar lines. We must remove this barrier, which is huge, or the consequences will be fatal. Some day, this barrier will boomerang and the Brahmins will be crushed by it. Those who are exploited today will carry out this unprecedented task. We need to be vigilant to avoid this extreme destruction. Yet another casteist strategy will be employed to attack this form of casteism. The most disturbing aspect of this kind of politics is that it targets the poorest section of society. The rich and powerful Marathas used poor Marathas to demolish the houses of other poor Brahmins, and the powerful Brahmins employed poor Brahmins to resist the strong Marathas. The rich and powerful of any caste have always been safer. Even when attacked, the attacks haven't affected them. The bitter truth is that the subjugated classes of India are unable to identify their enemy. But one finds Golwalkar quoting from the *Bhagvad Gita* and drawing pleasure from the construct of Chaturvarnya:

स्वकर्मणा तमभ्यर्च्य सिद्धिं विन्दति मानवः ॥

(Through the performance of his duty, man worships the Lord and attains perfection.)

Society was conceived of as the fourfold manifestations of the Almighty to be worshipped by all, each in his own way and according to his capacity. [See pp. 73–4 for the full quote.—*Ed.*]

In which era did this form of Chaturvarnya come into existence? Neither Golwalkar nor the Hinduists give any details. What were the criteria to determine social status? The Hinduist finds it a problem to answer such questions. Indian thinkers began to subscribe to a deceptive idea—that the social status of an individual was not determined by the wealth they possessed. This was useful to generate caste clashes between people and avoid a class struggle. It was useful for the higher classes of society to give currency to such ideas, as it safeguarded their selfish ends.

Golwalkar blames others, i.e. the non-Brahmins, but deceptively agrees that *varna vyavastha* (class order) is casteism:

> The other main feature that distinguished our society was the *Varna-Vyavastha*. But today it is dubbed 'casteism' and scoffed at. Our people have come to feel that the mere mention of *Varna-Vyavastha* is something derogatory. They often mistake the social order implied in it for social discrimination.

But Golwalkar does not want to annihilate the caste system. On the contrary, he endorses the caste system and says that people are led to believe that *varna vyavastha* and casteism are the same. He says that people often misunderstand it as an order of social discrimination.

From this perspective, Golwalkar has committed two serious errors in terms of historical analysis when he illustrates the power struggles of historical rulers like Prithviraj, Shivaji and the Peshwas. His first error is the contention that when these kings ruled, Indian society was composed of classes. Golwalkar has either not understood the class contradictions of society or he might not have paid enough attention to the contradictions. His other error is that to justify the institution of caste he argues that Prithviraj, Shivaji and the Peshwas were each opposed by people who belonged to their own castes. To support his argument in favour of caste, he says that those who offered their loyalty to Prithviraj, Shivaji and the Peshwas were not members of the rulers' castes but were from other castes—King Shivaji was supported by non-Marathas, the Peshwas were supported by non-Brahmins, and so was Prithviraj by non-Rajputs. Golwalkar's justification is premised upon these assumptions. The supporting details are misleading and they cannot stand as legitimate historical proof.

Did the clashes that took place between the castes, and within the castes, strengthen the unity of India? If yes, how? Golwalkar and Deoras must answer this question. Even though it is a fact that Indian society became divided due to caste clashes, why does Golwalkar glorify the caste system in *Bunch of Thoughts*? Golwalkar, Deoras and other Hinduists will not consider these questions either: Did Pushyamitra Shunga, the Brahmin who usurped the Mauryan Empire, belong to King Ashoka's caste? The Brahmin intellectuals in Prithviraj's durbar, Ramdev and Mahipal Jogi—were they loyal to the king? Did they not band with his enemy? To which caste belonged those who called King Shivaji a Shudra and opposed his coronation? Was Balaji Peshwa, who forbade the descendants of Chhatrapati Shahu from conducting the *munj* ceremony and took away their Kshatriya status, a Maratha? Nanasaheb Peshwa consorted with the Portuguese in 1740 and with the British in 1755 to destroy the Maratha naval fleet in order to subdue the clan of Angres, the fleet's hereditary chiefs, who challenged his authority. Was he a Maratha, Muslim or Brahmin? The Peshwa took money from the Nawab of Bengal and funded the Nizam of Hyderabad to defeat the Bhonsles. Was the Peshwa not a Brahmin? The brave warriors who supported the British against the Peshwa—were they Brahmin? The Hinduists do not pay attention to these details of history. This country has been enormously weakened by the caste system. It has been further impoverished by mutual enmity and distrust between the sub-castes. This has been the inevitable failure of the caste system. Peshwa Bajirao I, a Chitpavan Brahmin, was once prevented by members of the Deshastha Brahmin sub-caste from using the ghats while bathing in River Godavari in Nasik. The Deshasthas held the Chitpavans in low esteem. This led to a historic battle between the Chitpavan and Deshastha Brahmins on the banks of River Ghod (Ghodnadi) at Shirur. Everyone knows this history, yet why do people pretend to be oblivious to historical facts and ignore them? Why does Golwalkar falsify history to argue that caste has helped India maintain its integrity? It is shocking for a person who calls himself the leader of a nationalist organization to narrate falsified history of our country.

Has the integrity of our country been affected by clashes between castes or clashes within the castes? The Sangh's leader must answer this question. Caste has produced several day-to-day conflicts, and disturbed the integrity of our country. But instead of addressing this, Golwalkar argues in favour of caste. On the one hand he narrates stories and anecdotes to establish that the caste system helped sustain India's integrity, and on the other, he talks about how the enemies of Prithviraj, Shivaji and the Peshwas were from their own castes. Golwalkar is aggrieved that Dalits supported the British to fight against the Peshwa. In Koregaon, near Pune, there is an obelisk known as the 'Victory Pillar' on which the names of soldiers who fought against the Peshwa are carved. Dr. B.R. Ambedkar, affectionately called Babasaheb, leader of the Dalits, once said, 'This pillar is a symbol of the victory of Harijans over Brahmins.' With the support of the British, the Dalits fought against the Brahmins and defeated the Peshwa. Golwalkar describes the event as 'a perversity'! But he does not once mention the Peshwa's [Bajirao II's] perversion and oppression of Dalits. We can understand Golwalkar's attitude towards caste politics from these lines in his book:

> In their hearts [*sic*] of hearts, very few of these anti-caste zealots experience the sense of unity that can transcend the present-day perversities. Anti-caste tirade has verily become a mask for them to strengthen their own positions among their caste fellowmen. To what extent this venom has entered our body-politic can be surmised from an incident which occurred some years ago. There is a 'Victory Pillar' near Pune, raised by the English in 1818 to commemorate their victory over the Peshwas. An eminent leader of the Harijans once addressed his caste-brethren under that Pillar. He declared that the pillar was a symbol of their victory over the Brahmins as it was they who had fought under the British and defeated the Peshwas, the Brahmins. How heart-rending it is to hear an eminent leader thus describing the hated sign of slavery as an emblem of victory, and the despicable action of fighting as slaves of a foreigner against our own kith and kin as an achievement of glory! How utterly his eyes must have been blinded by hatred, not able even to discern the simple fact of who were the victors and who the defeated! What a perversity?

We must read the archival records at the Peshwa Daftar, Pune, to find out why Bahujan communities joined the British to fight the Peshwas. The Peshwas had harassed Dalits and Maratha farmers in exceedingly crude, inhuman and malicious ways. The accounts are beyond imagination. They raped women and young girls of Dalit and Maratha communities. The chaos was so terrible and menacing that our hair stand on end when we hear or read about it. But, like Golwalkar, the Hinduists of today justify the cruel Peshwas. They don't wish that their status as the controlling class be disturbed. Secondly, they consider all non-Brahmins as Shudras, and assert their political supremacy over them. It is a double game. They say that the four *varnas* are manifestations of God. But in modern times, there are only two: Brahmins and the non-Brahmins who are equivalent to Shudras. In spite of this, they argue that only they are the real nationalists because they are Hindu. Added to that, they trumpet the message that Hinduism is nationalism. Who can honour a statement like that? Nationalism does not exist in a nation where there is a perpetual climate of slavery, where the common man is continuously exploited in the name of religion, and where one wealthy class is parasitic and leading a luxurious and hedonistic lifestyle. In such a nation, the only '*ism*' that would sprout is the '*ism*' of class dominance and, in the context of India, it is the discourse of casteism! If the RSS and Hinduists are prepared to create an integrated India, it is necessary for the Sangh's chief to play a definitive role. He must develop a programme to liberate the crores of Indians living in poverty and must provide them with social and economic justice. We have to end subjugation in the name of religion, and we have to end the domination of one particular class over crores of poor people. To do this, we need to have a basic scheme for reforms and social and economic justice. Instead of offering such effective programmes, if you chant the name of Hinduism, how will it produce nationalism in India?

The spirit of nationalism is a spontaneous sentiment, not to be imposed by force. Unless India stands for social and economic justice—and there are widespread movements supporting social and economic justice on the principles of equality—and unless these movements emerge victorious, the Hinduist agenda is only a programme of Brahminical domination. Their agenda will produce

Malik Kafurs and Khusro Khans,[2] and on the other hand it will also produce the exploitative Peshwas. If our country remains trapped in the labyrinth of Brahminical hegemony, it will be completely destroyed. However much the Hinduists call it nationalism, it is in fact casteism. Some day, people will see the casteist face of Hinduism behind the Hinduists' rhetoric of nationalism. Hinduist organizations, with their people preserving their caste pride and their movements in the name of religion, are only worried about how to maintain their domination. These people will be responsible for India's doom. A majority of the masses in India are ignorant and illiterate and they are therefore naïvely religious. Inciting pride and ego may not be a useful strategy while organizing religious movements based on blind faith. Hinduists cannot rely on peoples' ignorance and their religious mindsets remaining the same. The process of history is dynamic, it does not pause.

Nationality cannot be acquired by an individual by the mere fact that he is born in a specific part of a contiguous piece of land. The ideals of life and the culture of a community must mould the mindset of an individual. Golwalkar agrees to this:

The first requisite for a nation is a contiguous piece of land delimited

---

[2] Malik Kafur was a general in Alauddin Khilji's army who led the Deccan conquests of the Sultan. He was a Hindu slave, a eunuch, who had been captured in Gujarat and brought up as a Muslim under Khilji's rule. After Alauddin's death he imprisoned the Sultan's son Qutubuddin Mubarak Khan Shah and appointed Mubarak Shah's younger half-brother Shihabuddin Omar Khan as the Sultan. He acted as his regent for a few months in 1316 CE before he was murdered. Following his death, Mubarak Shah took over the throne by ousting Shihabuddin. Mubarak Shah was later murdered by his general, Nasiruddin Khusro Khan, who briefly ruled as the Sultan of Delhi in 1320 CE. Like Kafur, he too was captured as a young boy and brought to Delhi as a slave (with his brother). Khusro Khan was a convert too, and some legends say that he was an 'Untouchable' before the conversion. He was captured and killed by Ghiyasuddin Tughluq.

as far as possible by natural boundaries to serve as the substratum on which the nation has to live, grow and prosper. Then the second requisite is, the people living in that particular territory should have developed love and adoration for it as their motherland, as the place of their sustenance, security and prosperity. In short, they should feel that they are the children of the soil.

A question can be raised: How can the existing social ambience produce love and adoration, for which an appropriate mindset must be nurtured in an individual? To achieve the objective, the social environment must be conducive for the desired nationalism. The thought of creating such an environment begs an important question: should a nation's structure be based on the domination of a particular class, or should there be an environment of social and economic equality? Golwalkar has answered this tactfully, saying that the Hindu social system is the only ideal system and we must therefore support the Chaturvarnya tradition. It is the only means to foster nationalism, he claims.

Brahmins have produced several *Purankathas*, myths, to establish the principles of the caste system and the notions of superiority and inferiority among varied castes. They have used metaphors from nature, like trees and animals, to assign inequalities among different castes of Indian society. While explaining that nature counts more than nurture in generating nationalism, Golwalkar narrates the story of a baby jackal nurtured by a lioness who attempts to run away from the foster parent after seeing an elephant. The lioness tells the baby jackal: 'No doubt, you have grown here on my milk. But you cannot help your nature.' Golwalkar cites the story from *Panchatantra*:

शूरोऽसि कृतविद्योऽसि दर्शनियोऽसि पुत्रक ।
यस्मिन् कुले त्वमुत्पन्नः गजस्तत्र न हन्यते ॥

(Doubtless, you are brave, adept at learning, handsome to look at, but the species in which you are born is not the one that can kill an elephant.)

The story, which covertly exhibits the ideas of superiority and inferiority, illustrates Golwalkar's view that any foreigner living in India needs to assimilate the ancient traditions of this country. The metaphors are pretty bizarre as the two animals compared are biologically different from each other. What can we say about such regressive thinking? It is not that Golwalkar does not understand it or that he doesn't have enough sense. He has a bachelor's degree in Science and he has taught the subject for several years. So, how can it be that an educated man does not have a sense of comparison? In truth, although he is aware of those facts, he accepts a version of inequality. To what extent do such evil ideas sustain in his mind while he hides them in the name of nationalism?

Golwalkar is attracted to countries like America, England, Japan and Germany. He cites the examples of these countries to support his vision of a Hindu nation. He ignores the fact that Western nations are not theocracies; they were not founded on the basis of religion. Believing in a national personality is different from declaring faith in religious sentiments. To submit oneself completely to a nation's priestly class is an entirely different matter. Even though Mahatma Gandhi, Jawaharlal Nehru, Maulana Azad, Dr. B.R. Ambedkar, and even Vinayak Damodar Savarkar were religious, they did not accept theocratic rule. In the US, it is not obligatory for a citizen to necessarily be a Christian. Russia and China officially do not believe in religion; in fact, they shun religious sentiments. France, Germany, the United Kingdom and Japan are secular countries. But a non-Brahmin officer should bow down to a Brahmin peon in the Hindu social system. There are only two communities in the world that are incited and blinded by religious convictions and sentiments—Hindus and Muslims. They require their nationalism to be supported by religion. The two religions may have diverse social and cultural structures, but fundamentally speaking, there is not much difference between them.

The mask of nationalism worn by the RSS disguises its casteism. This is evident because until now the organization has not done anything for the common man. In the modern world, character is neither built by using sticks and brandishing them in the air, nor by celebrating festivals like Guru Poornima[3] or by tying a Rakhi.[4] Several followers of the Sangh do not believe in these rituals but they follow them. The rituals are designed to gather people together and spread the idea of nationalism. So, the question that remains is: what must the progressive groups who never sloganeered about nationalism do to mobilize people? The answer is to correctly interpret the nationalism of the RSS, and define their own nationalism—human-centric, secular, socialist nationalism. Misconceptions about nationalism have been created among the people, especially youth, through sentimental appeals and media propaganda by the Hinduists. This needs to be briefly addressed.

The ideology of nationalism was promoted after the French Revolution in the late eighteenth century. By the twentieth century, the idea was reduced to a narrow construct in Germany, where it mutated into a dogma, supporting racism and ethnocentrism. Those who support racist beliefs or casteism, and firmly believe in controlling a particular class, have a profound interest in Hitler.

---

[3] A day when gurus, or teachers, are honoured and celebrated by their students.

[4] A rakhi is a thread, or band, tied by sisters on the wrists of their brothers on the occasion of the Raksha Bandhan festival. The thread symbolizes a brother's responsibility in the protection and care of his sister—which she acknowledges through the ritual tying of the rakhi.

Marxism disapproves of such nationalism and states that religious and/or racial nationalism are symbols of exploitation. Russia, China, and [erstwhile] Yugoslavia are some outstanding examples that show how these forms of nationalism are not found in many communist countries. The progressive movements in India do not subscribe to these forms of nationalism either. It is also true that these movements do not believe in a nationalism based on prejudice (like the Sangh's). Nationalist ideology involves a process of psychological manipulation. Democratic socialism does not believe that nationalism should be generated in people's minds by conjuring up patriotic sentiments through religious sermons or religious education. The Hinduist view that the character of an individual is built through the inculcation of values, what they call 'samskar', is not acceptable to socialists. Instead, socialists believe that the social system in which an individual lives forms their character. It is nearly impossible to build individual character under conditions of social inequality. Is it possible to produce good individual character in an unequal social system by making great efforts to minimize the intensity of suppressions? To produce character in an unequal social environment is to produce in a person the capacity to tolerate subjugation and harassment.

Democratic socialism believes that a group of live persons makes up a nation. The individual is central to the nation. There they have the freedom to resist injustice, reasonably express views against inequality, campaign against poverty and also counter suppression. The individual's freedom aids the nation's welfare. The aspiration for social welfare should exist among people through the generations. An equitable material basis that preserves human rights and duties and a society free from subjugation must be created. To produce such a system, you should consider socialist theory, which believes in the idea that human labour is the source of wealth. Those who do not labour will not be respected in society.

Socialistic thought guards against the inflammation of blind faith and superstitions in society exercised through public displays of religious rituals. It also seeks to prevent repression of people in the name of religion. It is necessary for the common people to have decisive control over the political structure so as to produce material conditions on the principles of equality and social and economic justice. The atmosphere in society should be free from fear in order to take account of the smallest mistakes and biggest blunders of the politicians in power. People must be politically educated to achieve this objective, and a social environment that is free of fear is necessary for this. People should know how to recognize their friends and foes in society. Unless social and economic justice are established in a country, a safe and happy life is not possible there. Opportunities to build character must also exist. If more nations become free of exploitation, mutual understanding between countries will also improve globally.

Numerous innocent youths from poor families who are working as paid soldiers between the boundaries of two nations are cruelly killed in the name of nationalism. In the name of international relations, is it justified to kill the poor who join the army? The rich loot wealth from the poor, and then to protect their wealth the poor are paid a salary to go to the battlefield and fight the enemy. After the war, the parents of slain soldiers are given a paltry sum of money. It makes a mockery of the brave poor soldiers who died to protect rich peoples' wealth. When social and economic justice forms the basis of a nation, people-led movements produce an awakening. Only then will people love their nation with positively charged emotions. In such a nation, the entire society, not soldiers who are paid like servants, will fight against the enemy. Love for the nation is not dependent on whether an individual is Hindu, Muslim, Christian, Parsi or Buddhist. On the contrary, it is stimulated by the foundation of social and economic justice in society. An individual's need for religion is a matter of personal choice. He or she should have the freedom to accept a religion and, by the same token, the freedom to reject it. It is almost impossible to produce a free, modern individual otherwise. This comprehensive perspective on nationalism, which is diametrically opposite to the narrow Hinduist nationalism, is entirely absent in the RSS. The RSS does not want a nation built on the basis of material equality. It does not want individuals who believe in the scientific temperament and reject religion, customs, and traditions. It does not want to acknowledge the idea that it is only through labour that wealth is produced in society. For the Hinduists, the nation is religion itself. Besides, they want the rich castes to be vested with wealth. They believe that power must remain in the hands of the higher castes and classes of the country. Thus, the RSS and Hinduist organizations do not want radical changes in Indian society. They are vehemently opposed to democratic socialism. Does today's youth want to embrace the RSS, which has a narrow ideology of nationalism? They must decide once and for all whether they want the status quoist, class-based RSS nationalism that breeds the caste–class order, or the inclusive socio-nationalism, which aims for socio-economic justice to all in India.

# 4. HEGEMONY OF THE PRIESTLY CLASS

While discussing Hindu nationalism in *Bunch of Thoughts*, Golwalkar propounds some theories on religion and the state, religion and society, and spiritualism and nationalist life. He also presents Indian history from these points of view. Golwalkar mainly suggests that materialist philosophies, Western modern theories, and even democratic and socialist theories are opposed to spiritualism. Therefore, it is necessary to understand the major distinctions between the two views—spiritualism as implied by Hinduists and the position of democratic socialism on the subject.

Modern thinkers refuse to treat religion or religious scripture as 'science of spiritualism'. I have come across some writings by modern Indian thinkers like Acharya (Osho) Rajneesh and J. Krishnamurthy, and Western thinkers like Bertrand Russell and others. All of them follow the general principle that spiritualism is not a science but an individual worldview. It is purely a solitary journey and quest. According to them and many more modern thinkers, spiritualism is not entirely a science. It is possible to produce a 'science of psyche' with the support of spiritualism. In reality, spiritualism begins where this science of psyche stops. Psychology can play a crucial role because it can be the starting point for spiritualism. However, there is no science of spiritualism; it is impossible to think of such a construct. The simple reason is that spiritualism means life itself but not science! Words enable us to reach the core of our mind. Therefore, spiritualism cannot be understood as a science from any sacred religious book or scripture, like *Bhagvad Gita*, Bible and Quran. These sacred texts contain descriptions of human enlightenment in the specific era when they were produced. They document a study of psychology. Those who express faith that sacred books are documents of science are in fact defaming them. Spiritualism refers to experience which is beyond description. It means it is beyond any rational explanation. You cannot capture it in words and so it cannot be a science. A spiritual thought is something that emanates in the mind but the effect after such an internal awareness has to be felt alone; it is entirely an individual journey. While the above observations are true, spiritual speeches and explanations are usually not useful to the common people.

This argument can be explained with an illustration from the Upanishads. There is a statement in an Upanishad: 'Brahman exists'. Meaning, Brahman, the cosmic principle, is the reality. A common person might say, 'There may or may not be Brahman. What do I have to do with it? I have no use for this Brahman.' But a person who has studied spiritualism might say, 'Yes, Brahman exists. I too have realized it.' It is interesting to note that an individual who has sought to attain spiritual consciousness does not require any evidence from the Upanishads that Brahman is the reality. This suggests that spiritual words and explanations are neither useful to the ignorant and illiterate who have not experienced spirituality, nor to the wiser and knowledgeable persons. Then why do the religious organizations promoting spiritualism and culture fervently assert that spiritualism is a science, and that society should be constituted in accordance with this science? Why do these organizations demand this? Answers to such questions are simple and direct. Religious organizations do not have anything to do with spiritualism as such. They aim to create a theology of spiritualism to maintain vested interests and caste–class dominance. They interpret spiritualism conveniently so as to suit their class, caste and priestly hegemony. Under the pretext of spiritualism, they repress common people. They take advantage of their ignorance and illiteracy and expertly play with the religious sentiments of people. It is the only thing that they are interested in.

Considering the history of social life in India, it is obvious that there is no spiritualism in the Chaturvarnya tradition, which Golwalkar wants to revive with the support of Hindu philosophy. The real purpose in it is hidden and selfish—to maintain the Chaturvarnya Brahmin authority. Even though Golwalkar prescribes the ancient Chaturvarnya tradition in modern times, the educated Indian masses of today who have emerged from socially and economically exploited classes have become aware of the dreadful, evil and venomous role of that tradition in India's socio-cultural life. And they have refused to embrace the religion and its 'science'.

In fact, there is an awakening all over the world, and it is steadily spreading in India too, that religion is wielded as a tool to exploit human beings. Since religions have been appropriated for the oppression of human beings, the implication of religion is drawing the ire of our country's youth. Indian socialist thinkers like Acharya Shankar Dattatraya Jawadekar and Acharya S.J. Bhagwat have critically discussed theology, spiritualism and Indian history. It has become imperative today to discern the socialist understanding of spirituality. For several years, Hinduist ideologues have been engaged in a bitter discourse by arguing that democratic socialism's materialist philosophy is anti-spirituality and, hence, irrelevant to Indian traditions. Today, the young generation, which is well versed in Marxism, is enraged. But it would be erroneous to jump to conclusions about democratic socialism on that basis. Taking an extreme stand is neither good nor useful if you want to introduce an ideology in society.

Marx articulated a philosophy of liberation of all mankind from all forms of exploitation. He did not visualize emancipation of man simply on the economic level, but in every plane of exploitation, including material and spiritual. It would be unjust to reduce Marxism to economism. S.J. Bhagwat has thrown light on the unique relationship between spiritualism and rationalism. He says that spiritualism is not against rationalism. The development of intellect is not possible only on the basis of reasoning power or the power of logic. For intellectual development, you need to also have purity of emotions. This is the only deviation forwarded by spiritualism.

While discussing the place of religion in Indian nationalism, Golwalkar makes a distinction between Western and Indian notions of religion:

Here it is necessary to clear a misconception that has clouded our thinking these days. When words like *dharma* and spirituality are uttered, pat comes the remark: 'Why do you bring religion into politics?' This question stems from a misunderstanding of our concept of *dharma* and confusing it with the Western concept of religion. The Western countries suffered for centuries because of their dogmatic concept of religion and the control of the state by the church. Our concept of *dharma* is as different from that as cheese is from chalk. *Dharma* or spirituality is not a dogma but a view of life in its totality. It is not a separate sphere of national life just as political or economic spheres. Spirituality is, in our view, a comprehensive vision of life that should inform and elevate and correlate all fields of society for the fulfilment of human life in all its facets.

Will Golwalkar's interpretation and analysis, and the differences that he assumes exist between Indian and Western religions, withstand a scrutiny of history? It is not appropriate to differentiate between Hindu *dharma* and other religions. The fundamental concepts like existence of God, soul, rebirth, and dogmatism are common to almost all religions of the world, with some differences. Golwalkar's argument is true that Western religious institutions controlled political institutions throughout history. According to him, religious institutions and priests did not take control of political institutions in India. But is that true? It is unfortunate for Golwalkar that Indian history has borne witness to the control of political power by Hindu religion and its priests. Soon after the priestly classes organized themselves, they began to exert control over the existing political institutions. This is the history of the world, and Indian history is no exception in that respect. It is therefore necessary to discuss some historical details at length.

The Vedic period was a transitional era in ancient India. It was a time when Indian society was gradually shifting from a primitive, savage life to a civilized state. It was in this age that traditions like the enslavement of natives were introduced. The conflicts that took place between the Aryans who came to India from the north and the natives of India, the Dasa, Dasyu and Pani, are described in the Rig Veda.[1] The fair-skinned Aryans who were settled in northern parts of India unhesitatingly massacred the dark Indian natives. Hindu texts like *Manusmruti*, *Parashara Smruti* and Chanakya's *Arthashastra* give details about the era of enslavement in ancient Indian history. There are innumerable instances described in Hindu scriptures of how the Dasas were enslaved—they were held captive after war, found when hunting for food, bought from others, and found in the streets, apart from those who were hereditary slaves. The scriptures not only mention the Dasas, but they also classify them in a system and lay down rules and laws for them. Besides, a variety of wretched punishments and penances for the Dasas

---

[1] The *Ruchas* 4-16-13, 4-30-15, 7-99-5, 2-14-7, 6-26-6, 8-96-13, 1-130-8, etc. of the Rig Veda describe these conflicts.

found transgressing the rules are also listed in the texts.

It is possible to argue that the Brahmin community may have emerged in the Vedic era, during the phase when conflicts between Aryans, Dasas and the Pani had mitigated, and when they must have started coexisting. Nevertheless, a long period may have passed by the time the Aryans and non-Aryans began to live together. There must have been cultural interaction and exchange between the Aryans and the Dasas, including forms of worship. Of Rig Veda's 1,017 *suktas*, which are believed to be hymns of divine origin in praise of gods and goddesses, only 40 *suktas* are not expressions of devotion. Who does not like to receive praise and admiration? When man is infatuated by them, then why not gods and goddesses? We find immense devotion for them in Rig Veda. The Rig Veda is considered to be a tool to learn ancient history because it consists of the panegyric *stutis*, which are composed by devotees. Similarly, the text is an important source of prayers to the gods. It is a collection of *stotras*, the prayers that glorify gods and seek material pleasure and happiness. It was the Brahmins who chanted the *stotras*.

During that era, there was a tradition of keeping *agni*, a fire kept kindled all the time. A space was designated for it, and in the course of time, the responsibility of maintaining the *agni* was given to a particular family. This form of division of labour became widespread. As a result, other families did not have to worry about maintaining the *agni*. However, the tradition gave birth to the priestly class, from which the priestly Brahmin family originated.

Some scholars believe that a priestly class existed among the Dasas, Dasyus and Pani in the pre-Aryan era. However, the significance of priestly families grew in the Aryan time. The Brahmins gradually settled down and received social prestige and distinction. It was then that the era of exploitation of the common people was born. In the beginning, concepts such as rebirth and the law of Karma were introduced, and a form of psychic prison was created for the common people. In fact, we do not find traces of those concepts in the Rig Vedic era. The reason being, society and religion were at a primitive stage in that era. It was a time when people were preoccupied by nature, and they were yet to become civilized. The Brahmins produced this psychic prison, and it existed in the era of the Upanishads and the times that followed it. It was when classes were created in society. Once formed, it was natural for one class to exploit the other. Brahmins began to exploit the other classes in this era.

The practice of *yadnya*, or *yajna*, fire ceremonies for sacrificial offerings, grew into a prevalent tradition. The responsibility of the practice belonged to a few distinguished Brahmin families. The families who performed the *agnihotra*, an earlier tradition of ceremonial fires, took over the *yadnya* practice and they became an independent entity. Although *yadnya* began primarily as a social tradition, in the course of history there emerged several types of *yadnya*, which went beyond social ritual. When, for their own welfare other classes became patrons, or *yajamanas*, of *yadnya* rites, the Brahmins began to take *dakshina*, or donation, from them. The first act of social and economic domination by the priestly class began at this historical juncture. It marked the beginning of material exploitation of the masses.

Between the Vedic and post-Vedic eras, many conventions emerged for the practice of *yadnya* rites. At first, the number of priests required to perform a *yadnya* was four. Later, the figure was determined by the economic status of those who wished to host the *yadnya*. Among the priests, the one who chanted the *ruchas* from the Rig Veda was called Hota. The priest who performed the rites and supervised the ceremony was called Brahma. The priest who organized and maintained the ceremony according to Yajur Veda conventions was called Adhvaryu. The one who chanted the *mantras* as per Sama Veda norms was called Udgata.

Then, from one *yadnya*, three categories were created. Of them, the first, *paka yadnya*, incurred minimum cost and required only offerings of cooked food. The *havir yadnya* was more elaborate and required offerings of oil, milk, butter, grains, and honey, etc. The third, *soma yadnya*, was only for the rich. These could go on from one day up to twelve days. About sixteen *rutwij*, priests, would perform it. Then the number of Brahmins performing such *yadnyas* increased from twenty-one to a hundred. *Soma yadnyas* included the *yadnyas* like *agnistom*, *vajpeya* and *kuru vajpeya*. Of these, the *vajpeya yadnya* could only be commissioned by Brahmins and Kshatriyas. *Yadnyas* like *rajasuya*, *ashvamedha* and *gavamayana* fell into this category. The *rajasuya yadnya* was meant only for the Kshatriya kings, and the ritual could go on for two years. The *gavamayana yadnya* went on for at least a year. According to the Vedic sage Yadnyavalkya, a full granary that contained grains to last three years was sufficient to pay the Brahmins performing a *yadnya* ritual.

The *dakshina* for performing *yadnyas* persistently increased over time. For the *agnistom yadnya*, except the elder son's inheritance, the *yajamana* had to distribute all other wealth among the priests. Dogmatic norms and rules for different kinds of *dakshina* were fixed according to the status of the Brahmins. The donations were in the form of goats, lambs, horses, elephants, slaves, chariots and grains. Along with material donations, the daughter of the *yajamana* was given in marriage to the chief priest. Brahmins were literally looting people in the name of *dakshina*.

The plundering went beyond imagination when the patrons were kings. Large donations were most prevalent in *rajasuya* and *ashvamedha yadnyas*. For a *rajasuya*, every priest would receive 33,000 cows; his assistant would get 16,000 cows; the assistant's helper would get 8,000 cows; and every other priest performing in the ceremony received 4,000 cows. This was fixed in advance. In this way 2,40,000 cows were given away as donations to the priests. Cows were always a part of the transaction because they were the currency in the barter system. Later, *dakshinas* were also imposed on the relatives of the *yajamanas*.

Additionally, during the *ashvamedha yadnya* ritual, the Hota would be paid a *dakshina* of 1,000 cows during the first and third day of the event. Then, the extent of the land conquered by the king during the *ashvamedha yadnya* was marked out as *dakshina*. The Hota would own the wealth acquired from the non-Brahmins living in the eastern direction of the land. The wealth from the non-Brahmins living in the western, southern and northern directions of the land was earmarked as *dakshina* for the Udgata, Brahma and Adhvaryu. This method of division is recorded in the *Awalayan Dharmasutra*, which says that the property of the non-Brahmins living in all four directions would be donated to the priests as *dakshina*. So the extent of exploitation by the priestly class in the name of religion can be imagined from this.

The practice of *dakshina* facilitated exploitation of immense proportions in the name of religion. The Brahmins admired and glorified the *dakshina* form of transactions. We find their mention in the first and the tenth *mandalas* (cantos) of Rig Veda. The Vedas were declared to be *apaurusheya*, i.e. not produced by humans and therefore of divine origin. This trick enabled the priestly class to impose the Vedas on the people. In the history of the world, has there been another priestly class that played such a cruel and intelligent hoax in the name of religion to exploit the poor? It must be noted that the priests, to facilitate the subjugation of people, added the first and tenth cantos to the Rig Veda much later. Experts on the Vedas have concluded that those cantos are later additions. The Vedas were then used by the institution of *yadnya* to codify the means of suppression, to the advantage of the priestly class. The Brahmins of the ancient eras are an excellent example of how the desire for wealth can create unbridled greed in a class.

Golwalkar wants to justify and revive the ancient Indian social system. Therefore, it is necessary to have a clear historical picture of the system that existed in ancient India. This is the reason for extensively discussing the institution of *yadnya*. Another important aspect of the discussion is the perspective of Hinduism that Golwalkar talks about. He depicts Hinduist ideals in poetic expression, and so it is necessary to compare the texts with historical details. Golwalkar says,

> With this ultimate aim always before our eyes, it was natural that throughout our history we have laid great store by the qualities of head and heart conducive to the welfare of humanity rather than the amount of earthly riches that one possesses. The richness of heart, the purity of mind and the nobility of character have always been the touchstone of our values of life. The standard of greatness with us has always been one's inner, and not one's outside, possessions. All outer things come and go. Why should we run after those fleeting objects? We opted for a wealth which is the unique treasure of human life, which we can develop within ourselves—the wealth of sound virtues, a perfect knowledge and of sublimity of soul . . . [W]e find in our land that even the great heroes and monarchs have worshipped the dust of the feet of half-naked *sanyasins* living in forest without a piece of cloth. . . .

What is Golwalkar's argument? What is he trying to arrive at? To which era of Indian history does Golwalkar refer? If you ignore the very early phases of ancient Indian history, we find that Indian society was always divided into many classes. We also find, at the historical juncture when class emerged in Indian society, one class fed on the others by economically exploiting them. It has been a

habit among our thinkers to use Golwalkar's theoretical view—
which claims our social prestige is not determined by wealth and
financial status—against the socialist structure. So, this is the third
important reason for a wide-ranging discussion on the institution
of *yadnya*. The halo of social prestige that we find hanging around
the Brahmins of today is a result of historical ruin and its residual
impact from the economic exploitation of non-Brahmins. It can be
said that after the invasion of the subcontinent by Islamic dynasties,
the relationship between wealth and social prestige should have
weakened. But accumulation of wealth and the control exercised
by the homegrown *varna* system have been going hand-in-hand
since ancient times. It is most evidently seen in the *yadnya* system.

After the arrival of the British, the social status of Brahmins
was at stake. Moreover, they encountered several difficulties in
accumulating wealth in the name of religion. The institution of the
*yadnya* was almost breathing its last, and it became a question of
survival for the Hinduists because it was the oxygen on which they
thrived. According to them, the gods created the Vedas, and the
Chaturvarnya tradition is also of divine creation. We are also told
about divine incarnations in the *Bhagvad Gita*. Are we going to
restore that system? Will non-Brahmins and non-Hindus accept a
revival of the *yadnya* institution? Several such questions exist. The
chief of the RSS today, or the one who will lead it tomorrow, must
answer these questions in the light of Indian history.

Golwalkar has said that religious power has no authority over
political power in Indian history. Will history testify to this claim?
Was religious power in the West really different from religious
power in India? This issue needs to be examined. Today, a detailed
account is available to us of how Christianity was excessively
powerful in medieval Europe. History gives evidence of its
hegemony over political rule, but at the same time we also find that
its dominance was thwarted. Here, we have to pay attention to the

fundamental differences between the class of Christian priests and the class of Hindu priests. Once we understand the distinction, it will reveal several things like religious rebellion, religious wars and, finally, how they led to the growth of democratic processes in Western society and why such processes did not emerge in India.

In fact, uncontrolled power, whether religious, economic, political, or in any other sphere, is blinded by the selfish motivations of a class. A Hindu priest and a Catholic priest are an excellent comparison in this respect. A rebel like Martin Luther battled with the Catholic priests. He won followers and the sympathy of royal families too. In due course of time, in Western history, an ambience was created for democratization of society. But among the Hindu priests there were no rebels. It does not imply that rebellions did not occur in our history. In the era of the Upanishads, several rebellions took place, such as between Kshatriyas and Brahmins, and, later, between Buddha, Mahavira and Brahmin priests. But rebels like the ones among the Christian priestly class were never born. One of the primary reasons was that the Catholic religious leaders came up from the common masses, that is, from among the proletariat of Christian society. Because of this, Catholic priests were not alienated from the masses. Their relationship with people survived through strong bonds, and was built on respect and compassion. On the contrary, Brahmin priesthood in India was a completely closed caste in terms of the interaction and transactions they permitted. So, their relationship, connections and bonds with the common people were entirely alienated, which is why they did not have any respect or affection for the people. Hence we find tireless and unparalleled contributions of Christian missionaries for the welfare of Bahujan communities, whereas the luxurious life led by Hindu chief priests within the *matha* (their residence) had absolutely no relation to the outside world. This clearly highlights the huge difference between the attitudes of the Christian missionaries and Hindu priests. It was therefore possible for Brahmin priests to oppose in an organized way and sideline mass movements like the powerful resistance put forth by Charvaka philosophy, and those introduced by Buddha, Mahavira, Chakradhara and Basaveshwara. The priests also exerted pressure on the political establishment to achieve their objective, which was the complete doom of Bahujan communities.

We must begin from the Upanishadic period to understand how Brahmin priests controlled the political class, because the Upanishads provide us with this information. As discussed above, with the emergence of the institution of *yadnya* in the era of the Upanishads, Brahmins exploited Kshatriyas, who in turn did the same to the masses. The Upanishads were the first texts to record the resistance and reactionary protests by non-Brahmins against their subjugation by Brahmin priests. A wave of conflict arose between the Brahmins and the Kshatriyas. Kings like Pururavas and Nahusha fought against the Brahmins. The Kshatriyas are said to have composed a majority of the Upanishads, which is significant in this context. It is well known that the Kshatriyas' resistance against the Brahmins is recorded in the *Mundakopanishad*. The *Mundakopanishad* makes fun of those who considered *yadnya* as an important cultural institution. It describes people who followed *yadnya* practices to achieve social and cultural benefits as foolish. This Upanishad sharply criticizes the *yadnya* institution. A majority of Kshatriyas also rejected occult practices. There is ample evidence of occult worship and sacrifices in the *Koushitaki Brahmana* (Rig Veda), *Taittiriya Brahmana* (Yajur Veda) and in the Puranas. The attacks by Brahmins on the kings such as Vena in the ancient period, Bruhdratha Maurya in the second century BCE and Harsha in the seventh century CE are conflicts that illustrate the tensions between Brahmins and Kshatriyas. King Vena was a model ruler, but he was against occult worship—for which Brahmin priests killed him. Such instances clearly show how Brahmin priests pressurized the political power in order to retain their hegemony. They employed all forms of carnage, conspiracy and deceitful schemes. This tendency of the Brahmins was seen even in modern Indian politics, with the assassination of Gandhi.

In later times, Brahmins found it difficult to diminish the resistance from Buddhist and Jain communities. Mahavira strongly opposed *yadnya* and the Chaturvarnya tradition. He was indeed bold, and it enormously disturbed the Brahmins. Nevertheless, Brahmins devised an innovative methodology during the Buddhist era. Buddhism had succeeded in developing a wider network of communication, which defied the Brahminical elitism derived from Vedic tradition. Even King Ashoka provided patronage to Buddha's religion during his rule. Several kings of the time unhesitatingly embraced Buddhism. The priests played a trick—they proclaimed that the kings who were opposed to *yadnya* would have to forfeit their Kshatriya status. It was a strange declaration indeed! The Brahmins used Pushyamitra Shunga, the Mauryan army's commander-in-chief, as a scapegoat to kill the last Mauryan king, Bruhdratha Maurya, in the second century BCE. They thus succeeded in usurping the Mauryan Empire. The Mauryan lineage was reduced in status due to its Shudra origins. This was how the Brahmins avenged themselves upon King Ashoka and other kings who remained opposed to Brahminical hegemony. This unprecedented form of vengeance by Brahmins retained its power until Shahu Maharaj's reign in the twentieth century.

Lokayata was yet another strong and powerful doctrine that resisted Brahminical hegemony. It was based on the materialist philosophy of ancient India. It came to be known as the Charvaka philosophy. The philosophy was entirely based on empiricism, and it dared to reject beliefs such as the existence of soul, rebirth, and the caste and class discriminations decreed in the Vedas. Charvaka is said to be the first materialist philosophy in Indian history. It did not believe in Vedic gods, and so it did not endorse *yadnya*. As a result, it was declared that the followers of Charvaka philosophy would be labelled as *asuras*, or devilish incarnations of humans. The RSS maintains that the materialist philosophy of democratic socialism is incompatible with our culture. The Sangh has remained opposed to the democratic socialist state by propagating this idea. Golwalkar and other Hinduists have narrated pseudo-history, arguing that 'our religion is a spiritual religion' and that 'this religion never became a force to dominate existing political power', etc.

I shall give one more piece of historical evidence before concluding the discussion. A Brahmin commander-in-chief of the Mauryan army, Pushyamitra Shunga, usurped the Mauryan throne. Brahminical hegemony was in decline during the Buddhist period, and Pushyamitra made attempts to revive it after he came to power. His extreme actions in this direction drew few results. Nevertheless, his attempt to regain the declining glory of the Brahmins was significant. He established a strong rapport with other Brahmins and manipulated his connections to ensure there would never be any more anti-Brahmin protests and rebellion. The ancient text, *Manusmruti*, gained validity in the socio-cultural atmosphere created by Pushyamitra. With his political support, the scripture earned prestige in society. It was declared that the Kshatriya legacy ended with the Nanda Empire, which was overthrown by Chandragupta Maurya, founder of the Mauryan Empire. After the death of Bruhdratha Maurya, the royal Maurya family, which was a warrior clan, was reduced to being known as a Shudra clan because an ancestor of theirs was Shudra. Bruhdratha was assassinated by Pushyamitra Shunga when he was inspecting his troops. However, no one described it as the murder of a king; it was considered to be the killing of a Shudra! Thus, *Manusmruti* ushered in *Kaliyuga*, the modern age, with only two classes—Brahmin and Shudra. By implementing such a system, the priestly class, which enjoyed religious power, also conquered political power. After declaring Kshatriyas as Shudra, Brahmins continued the debate during the Maratha king Shivaji's *rajyabhisheka* (coronation) and questioned whether he was Kshatriya or Shudra. To settle the matter, Shivaji had to invite a Brahmin scholar, Gaga Bhatta from Varanasi, to preside over the ceremony. Shivaji gave him one lakh golden coins as *dakshina*, and he also distributed nearly the same amount among other Brahmins who attended his coronation. Brahmins championed the tradition of *Manusmruti* well into modern times, when the Vedokta–Puranokta debates shook the religious edifice in Maharashtra during Lokmanya Tilak's time. It was ignited by the denial of Vedic rites to Shivaji's descendant, Kolhapur's ruler Chhatrapati Shahu Maharaj, by the royal priests who performed rites for Shahu according to the Puranas instead of the Vedas. The pretext was that the king was not recognized by the Brahmins as Kshatriya but as Shudra.

According to historical evidence, just like Christian priests Hindu priests also controlled political power. The Hindu priests went a step ahead—they became the political power. Golwalkar claims that the Hindu power structure was unique and distinct when compared to other religions in the global context, which made Hindu religion superior. This claim is utterly false and baseless. In fact, religious power structures elsewhere in the world attempt to compete for their supremacy over existing power structures, and this shows their capabilities and limitations. Some occasionally succeed and some don't. As compared to other structures, the Hindu priestly class achieved more success and they sustained it for much longer. They also maintained their dominance by implementing different strategies. However, those interested in producing nationalism cannot achieve success by falsifying history. The Indian Hinduists narrate pseudo-history by using diplomatic language. The kind of nationalism they cherish is not pan-Indian.

The presentation of history in *Bunch of Thoughts* is both diplomatic and deceptive. Which era of Indian history was glorious? Without mentioning specific dates of this era, Golwalkar indiscriminately glorifies the culture, customs and traditions of India's past. While he works up these tricks, at every moment it appears that there is a display of subjugation, servitude, enslavement, ignorance and exploitation oozing from the corners of his mind. But the roots of these fatal and ruinous consequences are to be found in the *varna* and caste systems that were introduced through Hindu lifestyle in the annals of Indian history. Golwalkar does not agree with these observations. He holds Buddha, Mahavira, Christians and Muslims responsible for the degeneration of Hindus in Indian history. But how could the Hindus have escaped the process of deterioration? While describing the Hindu community as an inclusive community, Golwalkar awkwardly includes Buddha and Mahavira, but he is not able to position them properly. He cites a Sanskrit verse:

यं शैवा: समुपासते शिव इति ब्रह्मेति वेदान्तिनो
बौद्धा बुद्ध इति प्रमाणपटव: कर्तेति नैयायिका: ।
अर्हन्नित्यथ जैनशासनरता: कर्मेति मीमांसका:
सोऽयं लो विदधातु वांछितफलं त्रैलोक्यनाथो हरि: ॥
(He whom the Shudras worship as Shiva, the Vedantins as Brahma,
the Buddhist as Buddha, the Naiyayikas [rationalists] as Karta,
the Jains as Arhan, the Meemamsakas as Karma,
may He, the Lord of the three worlds, fulfil our desires.)

This view of Hindu society is commonplace, and it is frequently referred to in *Bunch of Thoughts*. Of course, this view emerged after the income of Brahmin priests from religious rituals of Vedic gods and goddesses was markedly reduced. The kind of society that is described in the lines cited above is probably from the period when Brahmin priests began to earn money by performing religious rituals of non-Vedic gods and goddesses. The ordinary character of Hindu society was considered superior, and whatever be the purpose behind such description, it is easy to deduce why Indian society did not become a society in the real sense of the term.

The field of sociology defines society as a mass of people organized to achieve a specific goal. The Brahmins devised cruel schemes and hatched conspiracies to maintain the supremacy of the priestly class. By causing distortion and degeneration of society, they were persistently successful in maintaining their dominance. As a result, Indian society could never qualify as a society. The present Hinduists describe Hindu society as normal with an air of pride. But in reality they believe that the teachings of non-violence, peace, equality and non-attachment by Buddhism and Jainism have been responsible for the deterioration of India! Did Indian society become sober, temperate and solemn due to the teachings of Buddha and Mahavira, and is that why foreign invaders succeeded? History refutes this. Dharmanand Kosambi has already disproved the Hinduists' objections to the teachings of Buddha and Mahavira and their alleged consequences. Buddha passed away in 400 BCE or so. Two centuries after his *parinirvana* (departure), Chandragupta Maurya founded his empire. It is said that Chandragupta Maurya was a Jain. However, while routing the Greeks from this country, the doctrine of non-violence did not prevent him from indulging in violence. His grandson, Ashoka, became a Buddhist, but he nevertheless took charge of a huge empire. But when Muhammad bin Qasim attacked Sindh in 712 CE, Buddhism as a religion had been obliterated from western

Hindustan. The domination of Brahmin priests had resumed, and it was strengthening. Yet, the foreigner Qasim, a young general of the Umayyad Caliphate, killed the Brahmin Hindu king, Raja Dahar, abducted his daughters and sent them to Damascus.

It was nearly a century after the Muslims conquered Sindh and some regions of Punjab that Shankaracharya came into the picture. His philosophy prohibited the Shudras from studying the Vedas. And if they happened to hear the Vedic *mantras*, molten lead was to be poured into their ears; if they chanted the *mantras*, their tongues were to be slashed; and if they understood the *mantras*, they were to be killed. This was his Vedanta! Did the orthodox Hindus learn this from the victorious Muslims of Sindh? The Buddha was their enemy, but wasn't there anything to learn from him? The Rajputs were extremely orthodox and they did not believe in the doctrine of non-violence at all. Was it Muhammad Ghazni who crushed the Shudras, believers of the Buddhist philosophy of non-violence, as if they were the dust under his horses' feet? Or did that happen because of the Rajputs who were devotees of violence?

Brahmins held power during the rule of the Peshwas. Bajirao II was well known for his orthodox beliefs. He was also known for his violence towards his enemies as well as his own people. In the beginning, Daulatrao Shinde and, later, Yashwantrao Holkar, both feudatories in the Peshwa-led Maratha confederacy, looted the city of Pune. Should not the empire of these devotees of violence have expanded all over India? Why were they forced to surrender to the British, who were a hundred times less violent than them? Why did the Maratha knights surrender to the British soldiers one after another? Were any of them believers of the philosophy of Buddha or Mahavira?

Japan has been following Buddhism for more than a thousand years. When Commodore Matthew C. Perry[2] pointed a cannon

---

[2] Commodore Matthew Calbraith Perry (1794–1858) of the United States

at them in 1853 to force them to open their ports to trade with the United States, how did the Japanese people get activated into resisting the threat through solidarity and brotherhood? Why did Buddhism not turn them into a sober and helpless community? Vietnam is considered a Buddhist country today. The Vietnamese fought against a superpower like America and came out victorious. How could the Vietnamese despite their Buddhist background fight so bravely to achieve social and economic justice? Did Buddha's philosophy of non-violence interrupt them in their struggle for independence?

These illustrations clearly suggest that the factors for India's defeat are altogether different and have nothing to do with the teachings of Buddha and Mahavira. The Hinduist anger does not stem from the fact that Indians failed to overcome foreign rulers; the reason is more deep-rooted. Buddha and Mahavira fought against Brahmin supremacy and they promoted social equality. Besides, they succeeded in preventing exploitation by Brahmins on the basis of religion. This brought on the Brahmins' wrath against Buddha and Mahavira.

The Hinduists are happy to glorify Hinduism and Hindu rule. But why didn't they give the Hindu Pulakeshi his due, even though he defeated the Buddhist Harsha? Golwalkar has other concerns:

The Harsha–Pulkeshin struggle is sought to be made out as an attempt by the North to dominate the South and its successful rebuttal by the South. But Pulkeshin was not a Dravidian at all, much less a Tamilian! His kingdom was founded in Pratisthan—modern Paithan—on the banks of Godavari in Maharashtra. In any case the two kings came to terms and lived amicably. The North–South controversy is pure and simple power-politics got up by modern

-----

Navy led several successful naval expeditions, chief among which was that of 1852–54 for the 'opening of Japan' to the West.

politicians who find the present climate extremely congenial for sowing seeds of all sorts of separatisms.

Golwalkar's words sound fair. But the Hinduists must accept that the root of the conflict between Aryans and non-Aryans, and north and south India, lie in Hinduism and the Hindu social system. Those quarrels in the post-Mauryan period erupted when Brahmin priests plotted to snatch power from the Kshatriyas. Did the Hinduists and their followers ever use political power for the welfare of the common masses? Did they treat the common people with compassion and affection? If they had participated in their miseries and pleasures the problem of casteism in Indian politics would have never come up.

In this context, Bajirao II, regarded by the Hinduists as 'the ideal Peshwa', is a controversial example. During the drought of 1803–04, known as the Holkari Drought,[3] Bajirao II adopted a policy of helping only Brahmins. He openly denied his responsibility towards the welfare of non-Brahmins. The non-Brahmin workers and farmers who were affected by the drought, received assistance from the Parsi community and the British. The Peshwas, who talked about spiritualism, sacred scriptures, culture and traditions, did not come forward to extend help to the drought-affected poor non-Brahmin communities, even as a humanitarian gesture. The lofty words of their religious scriptures remained only words and did not turn into action. Obviously, the Peshwa's decision was based on the dogmas in religious scriptures, which state that in

---

[3] One of the first famines of the nineteenth century in India, the drought that raged between 1803 and '04 in parts of Bombay Presidency was caused by war between Yashwantrao Holkar and Peshwa Bajirao II. Pune and its surroundings were devastated by the drought, which occurred on account of the looting of granaries and destruction of standing crops by Holkar's army. Hence known as the 'Holkari Drought', it was at its peak during April–August 1804.

the event of a disaster or natural calamity Brahmins must be the first to receive assistance and aid. So, then, when the non-Brahmin working and farming classes fought in favour of the British, and in opposition to the Peshwa rulers, who was responsible for their actions?[4] Golwalkar and others are in haste to hold the British responsible for the disintegration of Indian society. But it was the Brahmins who sowed the seeds of disintegration with cunning intelligence for their benefit and selfish ends.

The revival and glorification of Hindu culture to profit a particular class is reaping dividends even today. The sentiment that this country does not belong to Muslims is pervasive in India. The Mughal dynasty is made into a symbol of 'foreign rule':

[The Muslims in India] are born in this land, no doubt. But are they true to their salt? . . . Do they feel they are the children of this land and its tradition, and that to serve it is their great good fortune? Do they feel to it a duty to serve her? No! Together with the change in their faith, gone is the spirit of love and devotion for the nation. . . . They have also developed a feeling of identification with the enemies of this land. They look to some foreign land as their holy places. They call themselves 'Sheikhs' and 'Syeds'. Sheikhs and Syeds are certain

---

[4] One of these instances is the Battle of Bhima Koregaon between Peshwa Bajirao II and the East India Company fought on January 1, 1818, during what is known as the Third Anglo-Maratha War. The Mahars, who were considered an Untouchable caste, had fought on the British side in the battle, after the upper-caste Peshwas had spurned their offer to serve in the Maratha army. The arrival of the British opened up new avenues for the Mahars, who had experienced untold injustices during the Peshwa era when even punishments were caste based. Twenty-two Mahars are said to have lost their lives in the Battle of Bhima Koregaon. Their names are inscribed on the Vijay Stambh or Victory Pillar in Koregaon that commemorates the battle. Bhima Koregaon holds a special relevance for the Dalits and each year they gather at the Vijay Stambh to commemorate the battle as a victory of the Mahars over the oppressive Brahmin Peshwas.

clans in Arabia. How then did these people come to feel that they are their descendants? That is because they have cut off their ancestral national moorings of this land and mentally merged themselves with the aggressors.

The word 'Mughalai' (Mughal rule) is used with bitterness in everyday conversations. It is the same tone used for 'Peshwai' (Peshwa rule), especially in rural areas. How can one know the depth of bitterness hidden in the word 'Peshwai' unless one goes into the rural regions of Maharashtra? The Peshwas ate the salt cultivated by farmers, raped their women, and left them all to die in the drought. When today's RSS mentions the revival of Hindu culture and Chaturvarnya traditions, it brings back to mind this history of Hindu culture. In it, one does not find any reference to the dignity of the common people. No references are made to social and economic justice and freedom by which the lives of common people could improve. On the contrary, a clear picture emerges that Hindu culture is the culture of priestly hegemony.

Another dubious aspect of the RSS as it works to revive primitive Hindu culture is its treatment of women. It has been discussed by the socialist and trade union leader Baba Adhav in his thought-provoking article, 'Sanghachi Dhongbaji' (Hypocrisy of the Sangh), published in *Purogami Satyashodhak*, a periodical of progressive ideas. Baba Adhav narrates a conversation he witnessed at the Yerawada Jail where he was imprisoned along with the veteran RSS member, Baba Bhide, during Emergency. This conversation, which reveals Baba Bhide's attitude towards women, would agonize anyone. The Sangh seeks to revive Hindu culture by insulting and humiliating women in every sense. So, it is important to consider the Sangh's outlook on women.

Across the world, wars have been fought in the name of religion, nation and race, and the warriors fighting them have been glorified and celebrated. But extreme acts of war, like the atom bomb that devastated Hiroshima in the Second World War, are haunting examples of human wrath and cruelty. Another instance of cruelty was in medieval Europe, where people believed to be heretics were burnt alive. In about a period of two centuries, thousands of anti-religious dissenters were massacred. But it must be noted that there was no gender discrimination in those killings. The responsibility of upholding moral principles and values, and preserving religion, spirituality and social welfare, was not imposed solely on women. On the other hand, Hindu women were told to perform *sati* by immolating themselves on their husband's funeral pyre under the pretexts of morality, religion, salvation and entry into heaven. This form of cruelty has no parallel in any other culture of the world.

In the *Ramayana*, Indrajit's wife Sulochana, and in *Mahabharata*, King Pandu's wife Madri, committed *sati* on their husband's pyre. Except these two instances, there are no references to *sati* from this era. It implies that *sati* was not a common practice in those times. According to researchers, the tradition of *sati* became common between the sixth to tenth centuries and afterwards. The literature created by priestly Brahmins sowed the poison of this perversion and resulted in centuries of subjugation of women. The *Aranya Kanda* (forest episode) of the *Ramayana* contains an adage that demeans women: 'विमुक्तधर्मश्चपलास्तीक्षाभेदकराः स्त्रियः'. It means, a woman has no freedom at all; she cannot aspire to be liberated or free. In *Mahabharata*'s *Anushasana Parva* ('Book of Instructions'), a woman is severely attacked and utterly humiliated with harsh and stinging words:

न स्त्रीभ्यः किङ्चिदन्यद् वै पापीयस्तरम् अस्ती वै ।
(There is no sinner like a woman; she is the most sinful.)

and

क्षुरधारा विषं सर्पो वह्निरित्येकतः स्त्रियः ।

(The blade of a sword can be balanced by snake poison at one end and a woman at the other.)

In a philosophical book like the *Bhagvad Gita*, women, Vaishyas and Shudras, who are described as being of lower birth, are called *papyoni*—literally 'sinful vagina', meaning, of bad origin. Such derogatory terms are constantly used. The *Parashara Smruti* too demeans women and states that women have eight times more lascivious desire than men do (स्त्रीनामष्टगुणः कामौ व्यवसायश्च षड्गुणः). The insults and humiliation of women reached a height in *Manusmruti*. Several scholars who had defended the tradition of *sati* were born in Brahmin families. Lord William Bentinck, the first governor-general of British India, tried to suppress this bestial and cruel custom of widows dying on their husband's funeral pyre. Bentinck was not only against *sati*, but also caste rigidity, polygamy and child marriage. With the help of Raja Ram Mohan Roy, he succeeded in enacting a law in 1829 to abolish the crude and inhuman custom of *sati* in the British-ruled parts of India.

Customs like child marriage and *keshwapan*, or tonsuring of widows, continued until the twentieth century. The economist, historian and educationist, Dr. Sumant K. Muranjan, has given sociological insights on the pressures of widowhood and the ban on widow remarriage in Brahmin families in his book, *Puro-hitvargavarchasva va Bharatacha Samajik Itihas*. Several rigid customs were imposed on women in Brahmin families, especially when a Brahmin woman delivered a baby. Women from other castes and faiths were not allowed to enter a Brahmin home to offer postnatal care. Only Brahmin women, typically widows, were allowed to work as servants to Brahmin families. That was why imposition of stringent rules on widows was made necessary—to safeguard the institution of the Brahmin family. Several details offer evidence of these practices. According to the Census of India

1901, in Maharashtra alone there were 15,500 Brahmin widows below the age of five. There were 3,25,000 Brahmin widows aged below fifteen years and 25,50,000 below thirty years. These figures reflect the strategy adopted by Brahmins to preserve the family structure. Despite seeing these numbers, what did the Brahmins do for these young women?

Just like the tradition of *sati*, child marriage and enforced widowhood conformed not only to Hindu socio-cultural norms, but also to the Hindu principles of politics and economics. Ramdevraya, a disciple of Chakradhara Swami has been highly glorified in the thirteenth-century text, *Dnyaneshwari*, which is a commentary on the *Bhagvad Gita* by the Marathi poet-saint Dnyaneshwar. It describes how King Ramdevraya's wife, Kamairani, was forced by his son, Shankardeva, to commit *sati* and turn herself into ashes on her husband's pyre. This was Shankardeva's political strategy to eliminate another heir with a claim to the throne. Nevertheless, while committing *sati*, Kamairani cursed him that his kingdom would soon turn to dust.

The third Peshwa, Balaji Bajirao (Nana Saheb), pressurized the fifty-five-year-old queen of King Shahu, Sakwarbai, to commit *sati*, as it was a political strategy in favour of the heir he preferred. While Madhavrao I was on his deathbed, he advised Ramabai to commit *sati*. The innocent women of this country, who were founts of affection and compassion, were forced to die. They were, thus, utterly humiliated and insulted by Hindu culture. The doom of Hindu culture is the result of these women's curses. All the Sanskrit literature that glorifies women and motherhood could not come to their rescue and save Hindu culture from deterioration due to wives who were burnt alive. In the mad pursuance of and immense greed for power and economic gain, the Brahmin priests could not even understand that the wife who died after her husband was also a mother who was glorified.

The economics of the practice of *sati* exhibits the extent of degeneration of the Brahminical tradition. It reveals its mean, vile and cunning character. The *antyeshti* ritual of the funeral required a woman committing *sati* to hold a precious diamond in her mouth and also tie five other diamonds to a corner of her sari. This custom was modified later, and a woman was made to commit *sati* wearing all her gold ornaments. Afterwards, the Brahmin priests would grope around in the ashes of the burnt body to gather the ornaments—it was only their prerogative. Therefore, the ritual of *sati* was indeed a golden opportunity for the priests. The continuation of this tradition obviously provided economic advantage to Brahmins. So they invented rigid rules and regulations for it, and created a halo of social prestige around the tradition. They constructed temples for the women who committed *sati*. They exalted the practice, claiming it was an example of faithfulness and the highest form of morality. In their sermons, the priests created a mythical image of the *sati* as a woman of power, and the same image was disseminated. To increase the number of *satis*, they encouraged the custom of child marriage, and a man dying without being married was deemed to be an evil omen. The priestly class produced a vicious cycle of entrapment that finally led the Hindu society to its decay and doom.

The Hindu leader and thinker, Lokmanya Tilak, was among those who opposed the Age of Consent Act, and helped continue the custom of child marriage. Can we afford to follow Golwalkar and say that the British rulers were anti-national only because they were foreigners? In what context should Indian women consider Lord Bentinck their enemy? Did Brahmin priests leave any room for women to recognize their friends and foes?

It is not that the desecration of women in the form of *sati* went unchallenged. Varahmihira, the famous astronomer of the sixth century, had protested against the custom. From the eighteenth to the twentieth centuries, reformers like Raja Ram Mohan Roy,

Mahatma Jotirao Phule, Gopal Ganesh Agarkar, Justice Mahadev Govind Ranade and Babasaheb Ambedkar had launched campaigns against the evil Hindu customs. Therefore, today's woman is free of those bestial Hindu traditions. What does the RSS say about these national heroes? How does it portray them? Projecting a false notion of historical unity among Indians, Golwalkar writes,

. . . [T]he diversities in the path of devotion did not mean division [in] society. All are indivisible organs of one common *dharma*, which held society together. The same philosophy . . . the same holy *samskaras*, in short, the same life-blood flowed through all these limbs of our society. . . . Diversity of sect had seldom caused bloodshed or unholy rivalry amongst our people in the past. Even while one tried to establish one's own thesis or while attempting to disprove the others there was never any breaking of heads.

How true is Golwalkar's claim of the greatness of Indian national history? Many thinkers have been affected by this misconception. In this respect, Indian history is not different from the histories of other nations—there is no reason for it to be so. Indian society underwent stages of development just like other nations did. However much you try to keep history static, it will not remain static.

Did not Pushyamitra Shunga assassinate Bruhdratha Maurya because he was a follower of Buddha? Wasn't the political conspiracy to assassinate Bruhdratha Maurya hatched simply because he was a follower of Buddhist thought? Didn't five hundred Brahmins plan the murder of the great Emperor Shilajit, alias Harsha, who was tolerant of all religions and creeds, but was a believer of Buddhist thought? This was recorded by the Chinese traveller, Hiuen Tsang. Is it false? Hemadri Pandit, a thirteenth-century Brahmin scholar of occult rituals in Maharashtra, killed Chakradhara Swami, who built the inclusive Mahanubhav sect, which was opposed to traditional rituals, superstitions and occult practices. Chakradhara Swami was assassinated just because Hemadri's wife attended the reformer's sermon, and a rumour was spread that the king had him killed. Is this story, widely believed to be true, false?

If Golwalkar wants evidence of 'breaking of heads', there are unfortunately several in Indian history. The Chola king, Krimikanta, did not approve of Ramanujacharya, who was the founder of the Vishishtadvaita (qualified non-dualism) philosophy. The king blinded Ramanujacharya's friend and disciple, Kuresha, mistaking him for the guru. After escaping to Melkote, near Mysore, Ramanujacharya succeeded in winning over the support of the Hoysala ruler, King Bittideva (later known as King Vishnuvardhana), who later became his follower. Ramanujacharya sought to put an end to the Jain religion by converting the king and his subjects into Vishishtadvaita. Some of Ramanujacharya's followers narrated with pride that many Jains were killed in the process. Was it not because Jains held a different religious view?

In more recent times, followers of other faiths and those whose views were different from the Hinduists' have experienced severe attacks. Innovative techniques were invented for greater levels of humiliation. When a procession of the Arya Samaj's founder, Dayanand Saraswati, was in progress, Vishnushastri Chiplunkar's followers took out a procession of donkeys. When Agarkar expressed a view at odds with the Hinduists', a mock funeral procession was organized. Savarkar, who is said to have been a rationalist, called Ambedkar 'polluted' for having converted to Buddhism. When Ambedkar embraced the religion, Savarkar roared, saying 'conversion is treason'. Thus, the history of India does not deserve to be glorified when compared to histories of other countries. The Hinduists must come forward to explain the so-called 'great history' of our country.

It is a riddle why there is no space for women in the RSS, which calls itself a national movement. Today, we find there are several youth organizations in the nation's political arena, such as the Rashtra Seva Dal, Yuvak Kranti Dal, Youth Federation, etc. But none of these organizations have shunned women, and women are not inadmissible in the organizations. They have not argued for independent organizations for women either. Why doesn't the RSS admit women into its organization? Is it because it does not believe in man–woman equality or is it because of convenience? The leader of the Sangh must answer if the organization wishes to maintain an exclusive existence of Hindu culture. Moreover, the Sangh must explain what difficulties could arise by allowing women to become members of the organization.

I do not believe that the voluntary squad of today's RSS, which wears half pants [now, full pants], and supports the Hinduist Chaturvarnya-based social order and women's enslavement, would treat women as equals. Considering the age of a majority of these volunteers, I feel that most of them are attracted towards the RSS because of the spirit of nationalism. It is a truism that the Sangh's nationalism is Hindu nationalism; it is based on the Chaturvarnya tradition, and, so, it is based entirely on the hegemony of the Brahmin class. Their reactions would be of great interest to me when they realize that Hindu nationalism is just casteism. Finally, the Sangh must show enough courage to discuss this history of our country in each of its *shakhas* (branches).

## 5. 'ENEMIES'

M.S. Golwalkar and his Sangh claim to be diehard nationalists because they are Hinduists. In *Bunch of Thoughts*, Golwalkar unambiguously questions the patriotism of non-Hindu sections of Indian society. On many occasions in his book, he also attacks Jainism, Buddhism and other non-Vedic religions in the Indian subcontinent, despite them being considered to be of Hindu persuasion. He bundles them together as one and criticizes them severely at times. Well into the twentieth century, Golwalkar continued the legacy of Hindutva (Hindu nationalism)—which has an ancient and long history. The historical formula of downplaying the rejection of priestly Brahmin supremacy by Jain, Buddhist and non-Vedic religions, but also including them, however reluctantly, in the Hindu fold is adopted by Golwalkar too. In his book, he identifies three major 'threats' to India: Muslims, Christians and communists. Of these, the listing of two, Muslims and Christians, suggests religious overtones, and the third, i.e. communism, has a political angle. What is the perception of the Sangh about these three 'enemies'? A detailed discussion on this is of utmost importance and a great necessity. To discover some answers, in the course of this discussion we shall examine whether the RSS is a religious-cultural organization or a political one.

When Golwalkar talks about Muslims, he brings up Muhammed Ali Jinnah's aspirations for Pakistan. He believes that while Jinnah was dreaming of the new country, he had also set his sights on Assam along with Kashmir, but his dream remained unfulfilled. Golwalkar describes the strong emotions felt by people of the regions that were snatched away when Pakistan came into existence in 1947:

> What are the facts? Is it true that all pro-Pakistani elements have gone away to Pakistan? It was the Muslims in Hindu majority provinces led by U.P. who provided the spearhead for the movement for Pakistan right from the beginning. And they have remained solidly here even after Partition. In fact, the Muslims of Punjab, Bengal, Sindh and NWFP which went over to Pakistan had totally rejected Muslim League in the 1937 elections. It was only in later years that, because of the wrong policies of our leadership, the Muslims there were pushed into the arms of the Muslim League.
>
> And again, before Partition there were elections for the setting up of the Constituent Assembly. In those elections Muslim League had contested making the creation of Pakistan its election plank. The Congress also had set up some Muslim candidates all over the country. But at almost every such place, Muslims voted for the Muslim League candidates and the Muslim candidates of the Congress were utterly routed. NWFP was an exception. It only means that all the crores of Muslims who are here even now, had *en bloc* voted for Pakistan.

Golwalkar states that in the elections of 1945–46, crores of Muslims, except from the border regions, voted in favour of Partition. At the same time, he casts aspersions on the Muslims who remained in India and wonders how they could have turned patriotic overnight. He also claims that the threat to India had increased a hundred times due to the formation of Pakistan. He says that hundreds of Muslims were arriving in our country from Pakistan to take over strategic areas, and that the number of Muslims had doubled within twenty-five years in such places.

He also believes that there are several Muslim power centres in India, which were countless 'mini Pakistans', from where several spies pass on information and data from our country to Pakistan, invariably through electronic media. Golwalkar complained about these and other things.

Regarding Christians, Golwalkar argues that the missionaries diligently propagate their religion with the support of developed countries. He cites a pact between Christian missions and the Muslim League:

> Some time back, news had leaked out in papers that an agreement had been reached between the Christian missions in our country and the Muslim League that the two should join together and between themselves partition the country, the whole of the Gangetic plain between Punjab and Manipur going to the Muslims and the Peninsula and the Himalayas to the Christians.

While explaining the role of Christians in India, Golwalkar says,

> A few years ago, there was an All India Conference of Christians wherein they were called upon to pledge themselves to establish Christian Empire in Bharat. And one of our Central Ministers was present there to bless the proceedings.
>
> Such is the role of the Christian gentlemen residing in our land today, out to demolish not only the religious and social fabric of our life but also to establish political domination in various pockets and if possible all over the land. Such has been, in fact, their role wherever they have stepped—all under the alluring garb of bringing peace and brotherhood to mankind under the angelic wings of Jesus Christ.

While reading Golwalkar's book, we realize that RSS

determined its policy regarding non-Hindus at the outset. But, as a diplomatic stance, it has been made to appear as though it evolved over time. Realistically speaking, the question of non-Hindus was resolved when the RSS was founded itself, when it was announced, or rather decreed that Hinduism is nationality. But it appears that it was difficult for Golwalkar to explicitly state it. To claim upfront that all non-Hindu people are non-nationalist or, at times, anti-nationalist, was obviously embarrassing to him, and it was also difficult to publicly make such a claim. So, he takes a moderate approach in the beginning:

> When we say, 'This is the Hindu Nation,' there are some who immediately come up with the question, 'What about the Muslims and Christians dwelling in this land? Are they not also born and bred here? How could they become aliens just because they have changed their faith?' But the crucial point is whether THEY remember that they are the children of this soil. What is the use of merely OUR remembering? That feeling, that memory, should be cherished by THEM. We are not so mean as to say that with a mere change in the method of worship an individual ceases to be a son of the soil. We have no objection to God being called by any name whatever.

Golwalkar tells non-Hindus to remember that they are children of this soil. He thus submits the view that conversion to another religion has destroyed their love and emotion for the country. While addressing non-Hindus, Golwalkar proposes an alternative by recounting Jawaharlal Nehru's words on national integration:

> Once Pundit Nehru remarked at Jabalpur that there was no reason why we should not be able to absorb the Muslims even as we had assimilated in historical times the Hunas and the Shakas.

Indisputably, this is the correct and the only way of integrating our national life.

This is our concept of Hindu Nation and our attitude towards the non-Hindus residing here—the only rational, practical and right approach.

Golwalkar stakes a claim on the idea of national integration and says that it conceptually matches the Sangh's definition of the Hindu Nation and its attitude. He calls it rational, practical and the right approach. Yet, he pleads with them to return to the fold:

It is our duty to call these our forlorn brothers, suffering under religious slavery for centuries, back to their ancestral homes. As honest freedom-loving men, let them overthrow all signs of slavery and domination and follow the ancestral ways of devotees and national life. All types of slavery are repugnant to our nature and should be given up. This is a call for all those brothers to take their original place in our national life. And let us all celebrate a great Diwali on the return of those 'prodigal sons' of our society. . . . So also we shall rejoice and offer our love and respect when all these brethren who have been wandering for so many centuries outside the house come back to our fold. There is no compulsion here. This is only a call and request to them to understand things properly and come back and identify themselves with their ancestral Hindu way of life in dress, customs, performing marriage ceremonies and funeral rites and such other things.

Golwalkar's plea does strike as sentimentality for a moment. But what compelled people to abandon Hindu religion? Was it by force, like Golwalkar claims, that the non-Hindu communities were converted to other religions, pushing them into a life of misery and slavery? Golwalkar is now drenched in tears for them.

Does he wish to suggest that when these converted masses were Hindu, they were leading a life of prestige in society? When the Hindu masses were seeking support from non-Hindu religions through conversions, what were the honest and sincere efforts made by Hindu religious institutions to protect and defend those Hindu people? When crises such as floods and epidemics struck, did the Shankaracharya leave his *matha* (monastery) and mix among the common masses, like the missionaries and people from other religions did? Was there no slavery in Hindu religion? Also, if these communities were to re-enter the Hindu religion, in which *varna* would they be reinstated? Why hasn't Golwalkar, who believes in the Chaturvarnya tradition and who has spent his entire life propagating it, explained this clearly? Most of those who converted from Hindu religion are Shudras and Dalits. If they were to assume their original places in the religion, wouldn't it imply that the number of Shudras and Dalits would increase in the Hindu religion? Golwalkar does not talk about these scenarios. There are only two classes in the modern age, Brahmins and Shudras—this is Golwalkar's view. It is the legacy of the *Manusmruti* and, therefore, the issue is easily resolved for him. This is why he did not find it necessary to explain.

Historically, three types of conversions had taken place in the country. As much as it is true that ignorant Hindu people were converted to either Islam or Christianity by guile, it is equally true that the people of this country were harassed by slavery, untouchability and humiliation. So, they preferred to embrace other religions, where their day-to-day life became comfortable. Even educated people of India studied other religions and thought them to be better, and so the number of conversions among educated people of India was more than a few. The well-known writer and educationist of Maharashtra, Vitthal Dattatreya Ghate, had said that a call from Christ was not only heard by the poet

Narayanrao Waman Tilak and the reformer Pandita Ramabai, but also by poets like Kavi Datta (Dattatreya Kondo Ghate) and Keshavsut (Krishnaji Keshav Damle). Tilak and Ramabai responded to the call, which they heard from within, and they were courageous enough to walk the path of conversion. Many other educated people of the country wanted to follow on the same path, but they did not have enough courage to do so. A noted thinker of Maharashtra, P.V. Gadgil, wanted to embrace Christianity but thought that it might be escapism, so he didn't. He expressed this view at a public event, demonstrating that religion was a matter of personal choice. The Hinduists destroyed the personal dimension of religion in their mission to politicize Hinduism. They floated the theory that a person who converts becomes an anti-national and an enemy of the nation. This notion is both irrational and horrifying. When Golwalkar cites in his book, 'There was but one true Christian, and he died on the Cross,' he clearly acknowledges the personal face of religion. Why doesn't Golwalkar take on the Hindu religion in the same spirit as he does Christianity? He does not talk much about who is a true Hindu. Had he done that, he would not have been able to distinguish between the two. However, because of their zeal to bring politics into religious matters, the Hinduists cannot adopt a broad perspective. If the fanatical communities of Christ cannot be called Christians, can we call the militant Hindus Hindu? Both obfuscate religion and spiritualism and both deny the personal nature of religion. They insist on making religion impersonal. How do they identify someone as religious? If non-Hindu communities embraced the Hindu religion tomorrow, would Golwalkar consider them Hindu? They may be considered Hindu for the sake of political convenience, but from the point of view of religion would these non-Hindu communities be recognized as Hindu? It is a difficult question to answer.

Strictly speaking, there is no relationship between patriotism and religious beliefs. In the Indo-Pak War of 1965, didn't Abdul Hamid, the soldier who was awarded the Param Vir Chakra, give up his life and become a martyr? Religious people are those who love people of all communities of the world. Those who consider Hinduism as nationalism cannot be held as truly religious. On the contrary, considering their background in scheming, extremism and conspiracy, they are people who contravene religion and spiritualism. Golwalkar's speeches can be described as spirited and brilliant. They are extremely effective and attractive, but they are surely not religious. On the contrary, they are essentially political. By advocating the theory that Hindutva is nationalism, Golwalkar turned religious sentiments into antagonism and he thereby succeeded in pursuing a discourse of fanatical nationalism.

Patriotism and religion are much-discussed issues in modern times. Stalwarts like Mahatma Jotirao Phule, Gopal Ganesh Agarkar, Dr. Ram Manohar Lohia, Pandit Jawaharlal Nehru and Dr. B.R. Ambedkar were the true rationalists and patriots. Equally, religious people too can be described as patriots. The Hinduists do not seem to accept this historical truth. A fundamental discourse on nationalism has been discussed by Acharya Jawadekar in his book, *Adhunik Bharat* ('Modern India').

Agarkar, a well-known thinker, discussed 'rational nationalism'. It seems that many, from Mahadev Govind Ranade to Jayaprakash Narayan, accepted the notion of rational nationalism. It wouldn't be difficult for us to accept it too if we were inclined to understand the distinction between rational nationalism and hostile nationalism. Rational nationalism is a secular discourse and at the same time it favours social and economic equality and justice, which is the basis of socialism. We cannot produce a nation by maintaining inequality in society and promoting Chaturvarnya. Equally, it can't be done through sentimental and emotional supplications in the name of religion. However, you can produce a nation by transcending boundaries of caste, creed and religion, and by establishing a solid foundation for equality and justice—this is the principal theme of rational nationalism. There is no reason for a rational nationalist to dispute the philosophy of spiritualism.

Nevertheless, rational nationalism is undoubtedly in opposition to those who whip up sentiments in support of religion, casteist exploitation and communal fervour. The entire generation of political leaders and socialists like Acharya Bhagwat, Acharya Jawadekar, Sane Guruji, Jayaprakash Narayan, Lohia and Ambedkar firmly believed in rational nationalism, democracy and socialism. It is a sad fact that this idea of nationalism is receding into the annals of modern history. The most depressing thing is that we are pushed into a state of amnesia and are unable to remember their contributions in this context. The main reason for this is the mockery by Hinduists of rational nationalism and those who contributed to it. Such developments enabled Golwalkar to go against democracy and socialism. Golwalkar wants social and economic justice, but he does not want it on the basis of equality. His concept of justice is based on religious relativism. He understands justice from the perspective of the Chaturvarnya texts, and argues for separate types of justice for the different classes, based on the Chaturvarnya tradition. A similar principle was followed in the United States through the legal doctrine of 'separate but equal', which justified racial segregation. In spite of its several practical difficulties, one can understand why Golwalkar was insistent on implementing Chaturvarnya so openly. The ideology of democracy is based on the concept of freedom, and the ideology of socialism is based on the concept of equality. Golwalkar opposes both. Socialist ideology is a form of rational nationalism, and so, it transcends the boundaries of the nation and applies to universal life. This obviously goes against the parochial and regional definition of nationalism by the Hinduists, i.e. 'Hinduism is nationality', and so they oppose it. The Hinduists have literally held spiritualism and Hindu scriptures as their benchmarks. Their favourite scripture is the *Bhagvad Gita*. The book does not make any systematic argument. It makes an interesting case for a very flexible and slippery philosophy, and one can pick up anything from it as per one's convenience. That is why, from Shankaracharya to Lokmanya Tilak and Vinoba Bhave, there have been contradicting interpretations of the *Gita*. There are several well-known critiques of the *Gita* by various scholars. Many non-Brahmin saints like Kabir, Tukaram, Jaidev, Chaitanya, and Guru Nanak were as accomplished as Brahmin saints—but they never needed the *Gita*. When we consider the saints who reached the pinnacle with the support of the *Gita*, and the saints who reached there without it, should we call the second set 'Hindu' just because they were born in India? When they speak in informal settings, the Hinduists might refer to them as Hindus, but then they will apply the criteria of *Shruti–Smruti–Puranokta* texts, the source texts of Hindu culture, and, accordingly, they will determine the superiority and inferiority of the latter set by class, caste and such other categories.

The ideas of spiritualism sown in *Bunch of Thoughts* appear redundant and of a more superfluous nature on the surface, but inwardly they are essentially political. So, *Bunch of Thoughts* is fundamentally an expression of violent and hostile ideas. Spiritualism and other philosophical discourses are like external casings of the book. Golwalkar's *Bunch of Thoughts* can be understood in a single sentence—he is not telling us about Hindu religion but he is informing us of Hindu politics. The distance that we find between Hindu religion and Hindu politics is the same as that is found between Islam and Christianity and their respective politics. Hindu religion is not different from Islam or Christianity, provided we eliminate from Hindu religion its emphasis on caste–class discrimination and Chaturvarnya. Hence, there is no reason for any difference between Hindu politics and Muslim or Christian politics. Politics of nationalism that is based on religion cannot be without fanatical debate. Perversion is in its character; chaos and anarchy are its outstanding features; and fascism its real face. In his book, *Shivratra* (1970), Prof. Narahar Kurundkar has presented a descriptive account of the conflicts between a Hindu and a Hinduist in the politics of our country. What are the reasons for such conflicts? The answer is found in Acharya Bhagwat's introduction in Jawadekar's *Adhunik Bharat*. Any ideology, including Hinduism, is transformed into perversion or it is distorted when it is alienated from the common people. On the contrary, any ideology supporting the fundamental questions of people's lives finally becomes a way of life for people. The Hinduists never came out of their casteist straitjackets and so they were alienated from the common people and could never become a part of their lives. In spite of the politics that they have practised for a period of more than seventy-five years, they have not taken interest in the problems, misery, suffering, poverty and the inequalities perpetually experienced by people. So, the masses have considered Hinduists to be a perverted group. Even today, the Hinduists are not prepared to review their perceptions. Therefore, there is no possibility that the Hinduists' vicious politics might improve in future.

When nationalism is distorted, it takes the form of fascism. It is true that such fascism holds an attraction for spiritualism. Studies have shown that fascism produces only perversion. Hence, in Indian social life, conflicts between the mass-centric rational nationalism based on democratic socialism, and the anti-people and hostile nationalism of the Hinduists based on Chaturvarnya and domination of the priestly class, is inevitable, and we cannot avoid it.

If the descriptive accounts of Muslim and Christian missionaries given by Golwalkar in his book are true, they are definitely unfavourable and they deserve to be criticized. No nationalism will be positive if its politics operates in the web of religion and, so, Golwalkar, who is himself an advocate of such politics, can only present these descriptive accounts in the way that he has done. According to him, Christian and Muslim religious movements are not religious in nature, but rather essentially political movements. Hedgewar and Golwalkar, who launched campaigns against Christians and Muslims, were obviously political and reactionary. However, they might refuse to accept this contention. This is why, while presenting his views in *Bunch of Thoughts*, Golwalkar appears to have lost his balance of mind. On the one hand, he presents an argument by supplementing evidence of ancient India's religious propagators:

> Our religious missionaries who reached distant lands in ancient times did not force their religion on other people. On the contrary, without negating their mode of worship, our great teachers tried to make it more sublime by fortifying it with an all-comprehensive philosophy to inculcate in them noble and chaste qualities of head and heart and make them better devotees in their own form of worship. That was real *dharma*.

But on the other hand, he demands that non-Hindus must '. . . identify themselves with their ancestral Hindu way of life in dress, customs, performing marriage ceremonies and funeral rites and such other things'.

Isn't this a self-contradictory approach? We find several such contradictions in *Bunch of Thoughts*. In yet another part of the text, Golwalkar says,

> Do we not know, for example, that even in the latest powerful

expression of Hindu resurgence under Shivaji, one of his army officers was a Ranadulla Khan? Later on, on the battlefield of Panipat in 1761, in that life-and-death struggle for the rising Hindu Swaraj, the key position of the Artillery Chief was held by one Ibrahim Gardi. With such historical evidence and national traditions for the past thousands of years staring in our eyes, how strange that some persons still say that the non-Hindus live in peril if the Hindu Nation comes into its own!

Ibrahim Gardi, a Muslim, was the chief of artillery in Shivaji's army. By giving such illustrations, Golwalkar shows that the Sangh is not against Muslims. However, if a Muslim candidate were to be victorious in an election, it is mourned. Is this not contradictory?

Commenting on the report of the States Reorganisation Committee (SRC), which was formed in 1956, Golwalkar expresses his disapproval of the committee's recommendations. According to him, our Constitution is a conspiracy to disintegrate our country. He expects the Constitution to brush away all the autonomous and semi-autonomous states and declare Bharat as 'One Country, One State, One Legislature and One Executive' without any sections based on religion, language, faiths and sectarian diversity. After claiming that the Sangh is not against Muslims, he contradicts it by objecting to the recognition given to religious and sectarian faiths. He writes,

The differences especially emphasised, and to a great extent fanned by them [SRC], were between the Hindus and the Muslims, the 'Dravidas' and the 'Aryans', the various sects such as the Jains and the Sikhs as against the rest of the Hindus, between the various castes each against the rest, more especially between the Brahmins and the non-Brahmins.

Partition is the most unfortunate phenomenon in the history of Indian politics. It is equally the most painful part of our history. The formation of the new nation of Pakistan at the same time is a separate issue altogether. It is easier to sentimentally express, 'How shall we forget the painful history of Partition?' But the valid measures required to avoid Partition were indeed very difficult to suggest and implement at the time. More than Hinduists, the democratic socialists of India were pained by Partition. The writings of Lohia reveal the anguish felt at the event. The communal tendencies of both Muslims and Hinduists sowed the seeds of partition politics. The Hinduists want Muslims to accept their domination and follow the Hindu mode of life and worship. They want Muslims to return to their original place in the Chaturvarnya. By retaining an independent religious existence, fanatical Muslims on the other hand want to bring back the dream of transforming India into an Islamic nation. Only extremists like hostile Hinduists and fanatical Muslims entertain such perverse and crazy dreams. However, if scrutinized closely, this nationalism is fundamentally a form of casteism.

Fanatical nationalism feeds on superstitious people. However, both, the Hinduists and Muslim fanatics in India, could not succeed in realizing their dreams. It is true that the basis of the social consciousness of Indians is affected by the inculcation of values, incorporated consciously for several centuries, which are responsible for India becoming a static society. The static consciousness of Indian people was the principal force behind the rise of casteist Hinduists and orthodox Muslims. We must also consider the democratic forces that were completely annihilated in the years preceding Partition. The impact of casteist Hinduists and orthodox Muslims on the one hand, and the dominance of feudal-capitalists in the Indian National Congress on the other, was markedly felt at that time. The democratic socialist movement was weakened because socialists had modest numbers, and it disintegrated further to a great extent. The resulting social and cultural atmosphere made it just impossible to rescue Indians from disastrous religious nationalism.

The democratic forces failed to take secular nationalism to the people. At the same time, people were not in the right frame of mind to examine what the religious forces had planned for them. Just as the Hinduists sought cooperation and assistance from feudal lords and capitalists in Indian politics, in the same way, the orthodox Muslims did not refuse assistance from rich Muslims and nawabs. We cannot neglect the fact that Hindu and Muslim capitalists and feudal lords nurtured religious contempt for their selfish ends.

The flow of democratic ideas became feeble during the freedom movement because of the capitalists and casteist Hinduists and Muslims, who attacked socialist forces. This is the principal cause of India's partition and the widespread religious and casteist riots that followed it. If socialist ideology had been strengthened, there was every possibility that the economic motive could have become more powerful than the religious motive in the freedom movement. The result, which was heinous, was that poor Hindus and poor Muslims ruthlessly raped women from each other's community. This would not have happened, or at least it could have been avoided.

The close relationship between religious-minded people and the rich remains intact in Indian politics. Both have a vested interest in helping each other. The religious politics of the Hinduists and the Islamists will continue, and the rich will support them. They will continue to keep alive the religious and casteist spirit in the people. The only way to shake off the stranglehold of religious and casteist pressures is to enrich democratic socialism. The socialists in our country have not paid serious attention to this issue. That is why they adapt to every contradictory situation, either in the name of internationalism or democracy. This subsequently feeds more contradictions and maintains the status quo, which does not activate any dynamism.

By considering Pakistan as an enemy, Golwalkar and other Hinduists take contradictory positions. Instances of self-contradiction are found throughout Golwalkar's book. The political organization of Muslims, the Muslim League, was formed in 1906. In the 1930 Lucknow Conference of the League, poet Muhammad Iqbal presented the idea that Muslims must have a separate and independent state. Jinnah presented an improved version of Iqbal's poetic vision in 1933. While the League espoused the idea of a separate nation, Muslims of Punjab, Sindh and the border areas rejected the League in the 1937 elections. Golwalkar himself offers this piece of information and agrees that Muslims in those regions did not favour a separate nation for Muslim communities.

Why didn't the Muslim League elicit a favourable response for a separate nation? And, later on, why did the Muslims support it during Partition? No one attempts to make a critical enquiry into this phenomenon to find the answers. Golwalkar holds the national leaders responsible for their wrong policies. But the tendency of Hinduists to hold masses of Muslims responsible for the wrong policies of their leaders is an incomprehensible riddle that remains unsolved. In truth, criticism and analysis of the birth of Pakistan as a nation have not moved beyond the religious and casteist conflicts. They ignore the material aspects of Partition.

Trapped in the sentimentality of resurgent religious and casteist forces, such criticism and analysis cannot forget the terrible sorrows of the massacres. Just as Golwalkar did not forget it, Jinnah didn't either. Was religion alone the reason for the birth of Pakistan? Or was it the looming fear of Socialists? Or was it due to the capitalists and landlords, who took advantage of casteist and religious prejudices? Did they consciously feed on such prejudices? Were the majority of the poor Hindu and Muslim communities misguided and deceived? These issues must be carefully discussed. Is the government in Pakistan today really a government of its people? Are we going to consider those people living along the border who refused to go to Pakistan as our enemies? The Muslims did not vote for the Muslim League in the elections of 1937, but nearly a decade later they did favour the League in the elections. What happened in the ten-year period for their opinion to change so drastically? The Hinduists shout themselves hoarse saying that the crores of Muslims residing in India love Pakistan. However, aren't there people of the mercantile and rich classes in India who actively exploit poor Hindus in every field? Muslims in India are anti-national and traitors only because they are Muslims, and Hindus are patriots just because they are Hindus—such postulations favour exploitation. While defining friend and foe, Golwalkar is trapped in a bind and is confused. The arguments he makes have no merit, particularly in the context of India's pre-Independence politics, when the leaders were keen to protect the interests of capitalists. They sought to appease the Muslims as well, and exploited religion to gain power. These are the important reasons for the partition of India.

Although India and Pakistan are two separate nations today, the basic questions of providing 'roti, kapda, makan'—food, clothes and shelter—to all have not been resolved in both countries. It is unlikely that these questions will be resolved anytime in the near future. They cannot be solved by religious politics. On the contrary, the intensity of these questions is reduced by religious and spiritual sermons. If Jayaprakash Narayan, Comrade Shripad Amrut Dange, Dr. Ram Manohar Lohia and Dr. B.R. Ambedkar had come together with their democratic socialist convictions and made a joint appeal for Nehru's support, we could have avoided Partition and the upheaval that followed.

Even today, the three countries—India, Pakistan and Bangladesh—exist as each other's enemies in the subcontinent. Religious nationalism has always been a threat and menace to these countries. But the people of these countries demand gestures of friendship and cooperation. This process has already started but without any direction. The formation of Bangladesh is evidence of the outdated value of religious nationalism. Will the Hinduists of our nation learn a lesson from this phenomenon?

Golwalkar suggests that like the Shakas and the Hunas, non-Hindus should integrate with Hindu culture. His suggestion is irrelevant considering today's situation. Historically speaking, the arrival of the Shaka and Huna, and the Muslim invasion in India, are different. The Hinduists are committing a blunder by judging them in the same framework. During the Muslim invasions of India, Indian society was in a miserable condition. People were exploited in the name of religion. The details of unjust religious practices have been discussed in the previous chapter. Have Indian Muslims, who receive contempt and hatred from Hinduists, arrived from foreign countries? Golwalkar is immensely hurt about those Hindu brothers who embraced Islam. But why did they embrace Islam? This question is not answered anywhere in *Bunch of Thoughts*. It implies that those who renounced Hindu religion are culprits. The Muslims therefore preferred to keep their distance from Hindu religion because of the evil treatment by Hinduists. But the Hinduists are described as blameless—this is the only meaning that can be drawn from Golwalkar's argument.

There is not a single mention of Brahminical occult practices and superstitious beliefs in Golwalkar's book. Such practices have bred a cult of inequality, which the Brahminical texts disseminated in the name of religion. On the other hand, there are plenty of references to *shrutis*, *smrutis* and Chaturvarnya in *Bunch of Thoughts*. And a clarion call is given to non-Hindus to join Hindu religion. However, they are told to return to their Shudra position in society. If they refuse to do so, they are labelled as anti-nationals or traitors. Is this not an attempt to sustain priestly hegemony through Hindu nationalism?

It is a baseless theory that the seeds of patriotism will sprout by increasing the number of nationalist people in the country. Nevertheless, if it happens, the number of Shudras will increase, and, of course, there will be plenty of opportunities for Brahmins to exploit them. The argument that if a citizen is Hindu they qualify to become a nationalist has no merit. History has proven it wrong, again and again. Although the Maratha naval armoury was destroyed with the help of Muslims, those involved included Hindus, many of them Brahmins who held the highest social status.

The rich traders and moneylenders Jagat Seth and Amir Chand helped Robert Clive establish British dominion in India by deceiving their own compatriots. They were neither Muslim, Christian nor communist. The feudal kings, moneylenders and merchants who helped the British Empire were Hindu. Before the arrival of the British in India, many Brahmins admired the rule of Muslims and stated that only Muslims displayed prowess during war. However, innumerable Brahmins displayed admirable sycophancy! The Brahmin military officers who tired of Peshwa Bajirao's eccentric rule joined the British side to extract the maximum material benefit. They were all Hindus. There are hundreds of such illustrations.

Do Hinduists dare to deny these historical facts? The corresponding evidence is available even now. The letters of the reformer Gopal Hari Deshmukh 'Lokhitavadi', compiled in the book *Shatapatre* (1850), make it clear that there is no relation between religion and one's love for the nation, community or society. Acharya Jawadekar has also argued along similar lines. According to Jawadekar, there was no connection between loyalty to religion and loyalty to the state in medieval and modern Hindu periods of Indian history. His insight is significant—it suggests that religion is personal expression and it is not connected to either the religious or social life of an individual.

It is not true that people who argue in favour of the idea that Hinduism is nationalism are unaware of India's Hindu history. But it is necessary for them to either hide it or distort it for their selfish ends or vested interests. It is delusional to think that burying history to hide it, or presenting it to suit one's convenience, will allow an escape from the historical truths. This pretension has devastated the lives of crores of people of this country. If you wish to create love for the motherland, you must first produce love for society and its people. And, to produce love for people, you have to build a society based on the principles of economic and social equality. The real question is: do Hinduists uphold the principles of economic and social equality? Have the Hinduists, who babble on about nationalism, ever supported the exploited peasants and labourers after India's Independence? Have they supported the land reform movement, when landlords gave up their lands? Did the followers of Hinduist leaders participate in the revolutionary schemes for social equality initiated by Ambedkar? Crores of Dalits and people living below the poverty line are leading a miserable and cruel life. Has any Hinduist taken a progressive step against the heinous injustices done to them?

Do Hinduists expect love for the motherland from all these people, even though they have been mercilessly exploited and have tolerated social and economic inequality and injustice? They are expected to be loyal to Hindu religion and culture and to sacrifice themselves for the nation. Which is their nation? Their religion and culture? Is the Hinduists' religion or caste *their* nation? Then what about those who belong to other castes and religions? Are they expected to respect and love the Hinduists' religion and caste?

It is obvious that the Hinduists are only interested in enslavement. This is the underlying demand: others must accept enslavement because the Hinduists intensely desire it. Will the impoverished and poverty-stricken communities accept enslavement desired by Hinduists? But, yes, it really happened in our history in the name of religion. However, this may not continue to happen in the twentieth [and twenty-first] century, when the values of freedom and equality have been underlined. Yet, we must be cautious, and prepared. In other words, we must take care that such enslavement does not occur.

Golwalkar categorically identifies his three enemies in *Bunch of Thoughts*—Muslims, Christians and communists. His reasons for considering them as enemies are varied. However, one aspect is common to them all—each is against Brahminical hegemony. From the perspective of religion, Muslims and Christians consider religion to be a tool of social equality, whereas communists believe religion is a tool of exploitation. So, communists look forward to achieving a classless society in which no hegemony exists of any class. If Muslims and Christians are really involved in religious politics, then it must be condemned. Although, the propagation of religion and the imposition of religious conversion are not religious acts in the true sense. They are political acts without a doubt. Therefore, just as many of today's Hinduists are involved in politics to sustain casteist supremacy and class hegemony—which is not only disastrous but also anti-social—so also are Muslims and Christians who practise the same politics, disastrous and anti-social.

Golwalkar does not make any distinction between socialists and communists. For his convenience, he calls them both 'communist'. Taking an anti-communism stand is a diplomatic move by the Sangh—it makes it easier for it to seek assistance from the rich. The Sangh has a strategic plan to make communists and socialists ineffective, so that the rich can be entrapped in a vicious cycle of religious rituals and occult practices, and made to part with huge donations in the name of religion—thus preserving their casteist goals. This cannot be considered religious; it is entirely political. Hence, the Sangh cannot be considered a cultural organization. It is obviously a political organization. We therefore have to bravely confront the Sangh on diverse fronts.

## 6. PRESSURE-GROUP POLITICS

What was the need for an organization like the RSS, which believes in religious nationalism and functions like a semi-army? We must explore the question in the context of the time when the RSS was formed. Prof. Narahar Kurundkar in his collection of essays on communalism and secularism, *Shivratra*, and Prof. Vasant Bapat in *Manus* (March 12–25, 1977) have attempted to explain this.

Golwalkar recounts that Dr. Keshav Baliram Hedgewar, the founder of the Sangh, infiltrated the Hindu revolutionary movements of the pre-Independence era. Besides that he also joined the Congress's movement. Hedgewar subsequently gathered plenty of experience of both these movements. He thought of establishing a unique organization that would overcome the faults and limitations of those movements by incorporating the motives that were absent in them. This is why he founded the RSS. The extremist path of the Hindu outfits and the moderate path of the Congress were both unacceptable to him. Hedgewar felt that he must start a new organization where he could apply his principles and proceed with his mission.

There is nothing wrong in conceiving a new organization when its necessity is felt. But what were Hedgewar's differences with Hindu society before 1925? This is not discussed enough. While looking at the politics of Hinduists, it would be incorrect to assess the entire band as one group—from Vinayak Damodar Savarkar of the Hindu Mahasabha, to the present chief of the

Sangh. Otherwise, it would be difficult to discern their diplomatic manoeuvres and discreet differences.

There is no doubt that the ideology of all Hindu organizations is the same. But the tactics and strategies that they employed in politics show that there are many differences between them. What were the views of the Hinduist organizations? They can be traced to the time when the Indian National Congress was formed in 1885. To understand the politics of the Sangh and Hindu Mahasabha, we must understand Lokmanya Balgangadhar Tilak's politics, especially in the period between 1895 to 1920 before Gandhi took charge of the Congress. The fundamental principles of the politics of Tilak, Savarkar, Hedgewar, Golwalkar, and the current Sangh chief, Deoras, are virtually the same. However, the strategies employed by each leader were different and there were many contradictions between them.

There was a shift in the Congress after 1920. Jawaharlal Nehru was moving to the top of the Congress leadership. At the same time, the wealthy capitalists who participated in the Independence movement because of its national reach felt that their relationship with the Congress was standing in the way of their self-interest. When socialist ideas started to enter the Congress through Nehru, the capitalist class went against him and began thinking of forming an alternative. The emergence of Sardar Vallabhbhai Patel in national politics and his power struggle with Nehru received the support of the capitalists. The Swatantra Party and the Jan Sangh were formed with the same objective—to provide an alternative to Nehru's socialist Congress.

Liberal ideology entered Indian politics in the nineteenth century with Mahatma Jotirao Phule's revolutionary ideas. Later, Mahadev Govind Ranade took them forward, albeit in a modest way. Hinduist organizations rose during the same period as a response to the growth of liberal ideas that were unfavourable and undesirable to them. When Rajarshi Shahu Maharaj in Kolhapur opened schools for non-Brahmin children and provided for their education, it gave impetus to the formation of non-Brahmin movements, which began erupting like whirlwinds. Consequently, contempt and hatred of Brahmins grew. The proliferation of socialist ideology and its principle of equality, was detrimental to the Hinduists. Although they were worried by it, it was difficult for the Hinduists to prevent it from spreading and to come up with revolutionary organizations. The wealthy class as well as the Hinduists were confronted with the transformative mood of the time, which created a depressing situation for them. They clearly saw that their vested interests were in the danger zone.

The Government of India Act of 1935 secured the right of an individual to own property in British India. With some modifications, the fundamental right to property was enshrined in Article 31 of the Indian Constitution after Independence. The provision of the 1935 Act became a tool for the rich; their politics revolved around it. During the Constituent Assembly debates, there was a difference of opinion between the socialists in the Congress, who did not want the proviso, and the group led by Patel, who insisted on it. It was clear that an anti-socialist movement was getting formed. What was transpiring in the Congress then makes it clear that the RSS and Hinduist groups were aligned to this faction. We cannot ignore this when we discuss the politics of the RSS and other Hinduists. The RSS, the Hindu Mahasabha and any such organization are not connected to a religious -ism, but they are in opposition to socialist thought. They function as pressure groups and are composed of the wealthy. The bond established between the Hinduists and the rich has been responsible for the increasing power of the Sangh and their aggression.

Whether Gandhi's assassin Nathuram Godse was connected to the Sangh or not may be a debatable question. But his allegiance to the Hindutva/Hinduist philosophy and its goals is without doubt. I have not read anywhere of anyone suspecting his loyalty and dedication to the Sangh. Godse's political journey is recorded in the book *Panchavanna Kotinche Bali* ('The Victim of Fifty-Five Crores'), by Gopal Godse, Nathuram's younger brother. The book lists the people who financed him, which includes many capitalists like the industrialist Jugal Kishore Birla, scion of the Birla family [his younger brother Ghanshyam Das Birla was Gandhi's benefactor]. Savarkar's biographer, Dhananjay Keer, has recorded that Birla would even decide the contents of Savarkar's speeches. That strong links existed between the wealthy class and the Hinduists is clear from these examples.

The Hindu Mahasabha is an important political organization of the Hinduists. The concept of *swaraj* was proposed by the Hindu Mahasabha for the preservation and protection of Hindu culture. It was the ideology with which the Hindu Mahasabha plunged into politics in the pre-Independence era. There was not much difference in terms of ideological beliefs between Golwalkar and Savarkar. In his book, Golwalkar even admires Savarkar's writings on Hinduism. Both these Hinduists held similar views on various subjects. For example, women. Golwalkar was against girls and boys mingling with each other because he believed that it distracted the boys from their purpose and was harmful to the nation. He said,

No nation can hope to survive with its young men given over to sensuality and effeminacy. This is the surest sign of decay and destruction.

In a speech delivered by Savarkar in Nagpur once, his advice to women was interesting. He told them that their responsibilities were limited to household chores and taking care of their children.

So, although both Golwalkar and Savarkar thought similarly about many things, one wonders why there was a wide gulf between their organizations. Not a single *shakha* (branch) of the RSS was opened in the locations where Savarkar worked. With an exception of one or two leaders, a majority of the Sangh's *swayamsevaks* voted in favour of the Congress and covertly opposed the Hindu Mahasabha. The defeat of the Hindu Mahasabha in the 1946 Indian provincial elections shocked Savarkar, who was ill then. The party lost in all the seats and Savarkar took the defeat hard. Keer has mentioned this in Savarkar's biography. What were the differences between the RSS and the Hindu Mahasabha? Were they in conflict over political power? Or were the differences in their methods and tactics to achieve their objectives? It seems that both these reasons could have been the root causes of the wedge that grew between the two organizations.

Although the Hindu Mahasabha was a Hinduist organization, it was primarily a political party. A political party based on religious ideology would have to tone down its chauvinism, moderate its policies on a practical level, and accept a few political compromises. This is true of any organized political party, even those with an extremely disciplined army of activists. The Hindu Mahasabha, especially after 1937 when Savarkar became its president, was preparing for several such political compromises. Savarkar would speak the Hinduist language in his speeches, but he would sometimes also speak about a universal world religion. After Independence, he permitted Dr. Syama Prasad Mookerjee to join Nehru's cabinet under the pretext that the new nation-state belonged to all. Not only that, at the Hindu Mahasabha's Nasik Conference of 1937, a resolution was passed that the Congress must preserve its national position and entrust the task of holding discussions with the Muslim League to the Hindu Mahasabha. The Hindu Mahasabha thus compromised its position by acknowledging the nationalist role of the Congress.

There are many such examples.

The Hindu Mahasabha, which functioned as a political party, accepted such compromises as necessary. But the concessions surprised Golwalkar and Nathuram Godse. They became disillusioned with the Mahasabha. So, when Dr. Mookerjee became president of the Hindu Mahasabha, Godse remarked that the organization had become a slave of the Congress. Golwalkar too condemned the Mahasabha on similar lines:

> The mere propagation of Hindu thought in literature and newspapers takes us nowhere. For instance, Veer Savarkarji wrote a beautiful book '*Hindutva*' and Hindu Mahasabha based itself on that pure philosophy of Hindu Nationalism. But once, the Hindu Mahasabha passed a resolution that Congress should not give up its 'nationalist' stand by holding talks with Muslim League but should ask Hindu Mahasabha to do that job! What does it mean? It only means that [the] hybrid nationalism of Congress was of the pure variety, whereas Hindu Mahasabha represented the Hindu counterpart of the rabidly communal, anti-national Muslim League! How did this strange perversion set in? Because, the deep-rooted conviction which would spontaneously evoke the ready affirmation 'yes, this is Hindu Nation' under all convictions, even in dreams, was not there.

The similarity between Godse's and Golwalkar's comments are striking. It implies that Hinduist politics is difficult to execute by a political party because of the many inner contradictions and compromises that a political party is required to make. This is why it is important to pay attention to the views of Hedgewar and Golwalkar, who seek to maintain Hindu hegemony in Indian politics.

The views of Golwalkar and Hedgewar in this context are therefore important. They felt the need to establish an organization of Hinduists in Indian politics that could stay aloof from politics, and which would sustain as a political pressure group in Indian politics. Thus, the RSS conveniently earned political mileage while claiming success in creating social change—at the same time withdrawing from politics by citing that it was a cultural organization. This stance was convenient for the Sangh because it alienated itself from real politics and avoided making compromises. Even today, the Sangh has not changed its double standards. It claimed success in the 1977 elections, but also denied its role by claiming that it was a purely cultural organization and not a political one. This doublespeak of the Sangh is not unfamiliar to the discerning citizens of India.

Golwalkar and Hedgewar must have given serious thought to how the RSS could work as a pressure group in Indian politics. Golwalkar visualized the Sangh as an organization where young activists from all political parties could be assimilated. An activist of the Sangh is required to be a staunch follower of Hindutva principles. However, he could work in any political organization or party. This was Golwalkar's liberal approach. It shows his plan for the Sangh's widespread reach in Indian politics. But the Congress did not allow this dream to materialize, and as a result the RSS did not grow into a huge organization. Following its victory in eight provinces during the provincial elections of 1937 and the establishment of its governments there, the Congress systematically transformed itself into a closed political entity. It imposed a strict ban on Congress activists taking part in the Sangh's activities. Golwalkar comments about this:

> The present perversion began setting in even as early as 1937 when Congress began tasting the loaves of political power. . . . But after Congress formed ministries in several provinces in 1937, it contracted itself into a political shell, prohibited its members from participating in the activities of the Sangh and introduced the new poison of 'political untouchability' in our body-politic.

Golwalkar's grievance that the Congress turned the Sangh into an 'untouchable organization', reveals his disillusionment. While reading *Bunch of Thoughts*, one finds Golwalkar severely criticizing Savarkar in two instances without mentioning him by name. In the first one, he speaks of Savarkar's political compromises on behalf of the Hindu Mahasabha. He refers to him as a 'reactionary Hindu' and describes his Hinduism as 'negative Hinduism':

But, unfortunately, what do we see all around us? Some are Hindus not out of conviction, but out of reaction. To give an example, our workers once approached a prominent Hindu leader during the signature collection campaign demanding ban on the slaughter of cows. But they were greatly shocked to hear him saying, 'What is the use of preventing the slaughter of useless cattle? Let them die. What does it matter? After all, one animal is as good as the other. But, since the Muslims are bent upon cow-slaughter, we should make this an issue. And so, I give you my signature.' What does this show? We are to protect the cow not because the cow has been for ages an emblem of Hindu devotion but because the Muslims kill it! This is Hinduism born out of reaction, a kind of 'negative Hinduism'.

On Savarkar's views on cow slaughter and eating cow meat, Golwalkar writes,

There is a revealing incident, which I came across during the anti-cow-slaughter campaign. I met a Hindu leader of great repute and scholarship known for his fiery patriotism. During our talk he casually asked, 'What harm is there if a Hindu takes beef?' I was simply stunned to hear such words from that person, whom I hold in great respect. What must have been the reason for such an utterance, which even the most depraved Hindu would shudder to think of? The reason is, the continuous thinking about the Muslims and their vices had left their deep impress upon his mind and made him culturally a Muslim, though he remained politically a Hindu. . . . It is this atmosphere of reactionary mentality that makes people view the Sangh also in the same light.

The severity of Golwalkar's criticism of Savarkar can seldom be found among Savarkar's opposers. Nevertheless, no *swayamsevak* of the Sangh seems to have given any thought to why Savarkar was compelled to take such positions. It is a well-known fact that to a certain extent the Sangh does not bow down to political compromises; it remains distant from real politics. Even if this were true, the Sangh's leaders reiterate that the Jan Sangh and Akhil Bharatiya Vidyarthi Parishad have been the Sangh's precious gifts to the nation! So, in the end, by linking the Sangh to the Jan Sangh, does it not imply that the Sangh accepts its participation in the nation's politics? Will the Sangh oppose the Jan Sangh for its political compromises like how it criticized Savarkar for similar political compromises?

Leadership of the RSS means the leadership of Hedgewar. In *Shivratra*, Prof. Narahar Kurundkar writes about Hedgewar, Golwalkar and the present Sangh chief:

It is true that none of them [Hedgewar, Golwalkar and Deoras] have received any traditional training or education to become a *mathadhish* or *peetadhish*, meaning traditional training or education in ancient scriptures. This organisation is not an organisation of the people who have trust in traditional religion. Traditional and orthodox religious people cannot be accommodated in the RSS. The Sangh does not indulge in village fairs nor does it encourage its followers to perform *yadnya* rituals, etc. The young activists of the Sangh are not advised either to go to Himalayas for performing *tapascharya* nor are they inspired to do rigorous *yoga* to become *sadhus.* This organisation does not insist on such Hindu rituals and rites like growing *shendi,* wearing the *janeu sandhya, ekadashi, vaishwadev, shradha-paksh,* etc. This is an organisation of modern young people, who are educated. They are assembled around Golwalkar Guruji seeking a pledge to protect the Hindu nation.

To a certain extent what Prof. Kurundkar says about the Sangh is true. It does not organize village fairs, no *yadnya, janeu* or growing of *shendi,* nor does it follow rituals like *sandhya* and *ekadashi.* Nevertheless, the belief that all these rituals are holy and must be religiously followed, exists among the Sangh's activists. Therefore, the Sangh stresses on the importance of festivals like *Padwa, Gurupuja, Raksha Bandhan, Vijaya Dashami, Makar Sankrant* and refers to them as 'national festivals'. Golwalkar writes,

> *Guru Pooja* (Ashadha Poornima) as [*sic*] the traditional day when the pupil renders homage to his teacher. . . . *Raksha Bandhan* (Shravana Poornima) reminds us that we are the children of a common motherland. We tie *Rakhi,* a symbol of fraternity, on this day. *Vijayadashami* (Ashwayuja Suddha Dashami) rekindles memories of the glorious tradition of our victories over the forces of evil. . . . *Makar Sankraman,* which marks the transition in nature from 'darkness to light', holds for us the message to emerge from the darkness of selfishness to the light of national consciousness.
>
> Thus on the one hand, the virtues of national consciousness, character and cohesion are infused into the people by the day-to-day training in the Shakha and, on the other hand, the flame of national awakening is fed by the various national festivals.

Golwalkar admits that the festivals are celebrated with the aim to infuse 'character and cohesion' and awaken national consciousness. However, the practice of these religious rites is unaffordable in day-to-day life. So one tends to give them up, and the customs and traditions often change with changing times. But this is not the same thing. Although the observance of such religious rites consume a lot of time in everyday life and they are often expensive as well, Golwalkar has succeeded in producing a good deal of attraction towards such customs and traditions among the youth. He consistently motivated young men towards orthodox ideology. But I don't think that Golwalkar has accepted the theory of Chaturvarnya for its own sake.

In virtue and conviction, communities all over India believe in spiritualism. A mind that believes in the Chaturvarnya system is a traditional Hindu mind. If you begin to count such Hindus, you will have to enlist the entire Indian population. Kurundkar's analysis that the Sangh approves of the *varna* system not because it feels love and affection for it, but to gather as many rural people under its banner as possible, is not acceptable to me. The reason being, democratic aspirations were instilled in our communities after the arrival of the British in India, and in the 1937 elections various castes supported the democratic forces. The signs of democratic aspirations were conspicuous. While an Indian may be a religious-minded person in general, in the quest for political power this religious mind is influenced by caste and the caste system. Bahujan communities consciously opposed Brahminical dominance to gain political power. This was true not only in Maharashtra but also in Tamil Nadu and Andhra Pradesh. It is possible to say that it occurred to a lesser degree in the north than in the south. In spite of this, a majority of the Indian population, though Hindu, did not support nor assist the Hindu Mahasabha and the Sangh. The reason was that the consciousness of religious-minded Indians was affected by the transformative political developments that took place at that time. However, such changes in the Indian psyche were also partly responsible for making casteism more powerful.

Kurundkar has not taken cognizance of the political strategies that turned the rural people of India against the Sangh-favouring Brahmins. Therefore, he naïvely misinterprets that a religious-minded rural community might assemble under the Sangh's banner. Although Kurundkar took the rural people into account while analysing the tactics of the Sangh, he neglected the fact that people in rural India today are more aware of caste and are more anti-Brahminism than their urban counterparts. Kurundkar imagined the rural folk to be naïve; Golwalkar did not. Golwalkar clearly saw what would destroy the Hindu Mahasabha and he knew the limitations of the Jan Sangh.

It seems to me that while embracing Chaturvarnya, Golwalkar did not imagine bringing the anti-Brahminical rural citizens under the Sangh's influence. He was certain that the upper classes would gather under its banner. His prediction came true to a great extent. The young people that rally around the Sangh today are elitist, and the rest are not aware of the Sangh's true face. I think that Golwalkar did not intend for the Sangh to proliferate across the nation. He did not advocate Chaturvarnya to bring religious-minded rural people under the RSS either. In fact, he did not want Hindus to crowd the Sangh. On the contrary, his Chaturvarnya policy is a strategic move to draw a select number of Brahmin youth into the Sangh. He consciously embraced Chaturvarnya because he was confident of achieving this goal.

In the course of organizing the Hindus, Chaturvarnya did not become a barrier but rather a practical tool in the Sangh's strategy. Only those who were required to be brought together came into the Sangh's fold, and the others were obviously thrown out. Golwalkar and Hedgewar believed that only a select few would produce the desired impact on Indian politics. Their policy bore fruit to a certain extent. They knew that they might even harness their power when the organization needed to become forceful and aggressive. This dream of Golwalkar's has not yet come true. [Nevertheless, at the time of translating this text, Narendra Modi's government had come to power and one can say that Golwalkar's dream has come true.] Golwalkar has ridiculed democracy and individual freedom, and at the same time pitched anti-social policies. This, in a sense, is fascist tendency.

The Sangh comprises of young people today, but it would be wrong to assume that the group is fully Hinduist. A large portion of its members are reactionary and negative. This is a result of the erroneous Muslim-oriented policies that our politicians have been pursuing in Indian politics. A part of it is due to the confusing notion of nationalism and its interpretations by the socialists and communists of our country. When political parties follow strong policies and sincerely implement concrete programmes, this group thronging the Sangh will automatically fade away. Only the Hinduists will remain then.

Golwalkar routinely compares Gandhi and Vinoba Bhave in his discussions. Superficially, there appears to be a good deal of similarity between Gandhi, Vinoba and Golwalkar. But we can clarify the differences if we regard them on the basis of two categories—those with a religious temperament who are connected to politics, and those who politicize religion. We have to consider Mahadev Govind Ranade, Mahatma Gandhi, Maulana Azad, and Jayaprakash Narayan in the first category, and Mookerjee, Savarkar, Jinnah and Golwalkar in the second. There is a difference between religious people in politics and those who practise religion-based politics. Those who seek to rule on the basis of religion fall into the trap of casteist politics. A comparison between Gandhi and Jinnah is significant in this discussion: Gandhi was a religious politician, while Jinnah used religion for politics.

We can see many changes in the RSS after Independence. But they are superficial and are merely a part of the Sangh's strategy.

Golwalkar does not accept the National Flag. The basis of the flag's tricolour composition is not acceptable to him. He rejects the explanation offered by experts and says that the coloured stripes are merely imitative of the French flag (which represents the principles of liberty, equality and fraternity). He remarks,

> Who can say that this is a pure and healthy national outlook? It was just a politician's patchwork, just political expediency. It was not inspired by any national vision or truth based on our national history and heritage. The same flag has been taken up today as our State Flag with only a glorious past. Then, had we no flag of our own? Had we no national emblem at all these thousands of years? Undoubtedly, we had. Then, why this void, this utter vacuum in our minds?

Indira Gandhi enacted the 42$^{nd}$ amendment to the Constitution of India in 1977. Reclaiming the fundamental rights of individuals that were curtailed through the amendment became an important issue. But Golwalkar does not accept the Constitution, saying there was nothing Indian in it. He says,

> Our Constitution too is just a cumbersome and heterogeneous piecing together of various articles from various Constitutions of Western countries. It has absolutely nothing which can be called our own. Is there a single word of reference in its guiding principles as to what our national mission is, what our keynote in life is? No! Some lame principles form [*sic*] the United Nations Charter or from the Charter of the now defunct League of Nations and some features from the American and the British Constitutions have been just brought together in a mere hotchpotch.

After reading what Golwalkar says about the National Flag and the Constitution, I remembered the controversy over what the young Dalit writer Raja Dhale wrote about the National Flag in his article published in the periodical *Sadhana*. Even though Golwalkar himself did not approve of the National Flag and the Constitution, at that time the Sangh's *swayamsevaks* harassed Shreedhar Mahadev Joshi, Yadunath Thatte and Anil Awachat, who were on the editorial board of the periodical. In their speeches after the elections of 1977, which they referred to as the 'second Independence', the RSS leaders stated that the Sangh had diligently fought to protect the fundamental rights enshrined in the Constitution. But this is not true. Is the Sangh loyal to the country's National Flag and Constitution? Deoras must answer this question.

Golwalkar had been a Vedist. He spent his entire life on reviving Vedic culture. By describing the National Flag and the Constitution as imitations of foreign flags and constitutions, he trapped himself into the straitjacket of fake nationalism, in a sense. It is indeed surprising that the prayer from Rig Veda—आ नो भद्राः क्रतवो यन्तु विश्वतः (Let all good thoughts reach us from all directions)—did not reach Golwalkar, the Vedist. Is it true that he did not accept anything at all from outsiders or from foreign lands? No. He accepted the foreign ideas that were convenient to his ideology, and incorporated them into his thoughts. This is evident from his insights, speeches and writings. To strengthen his argument against the Constitution he borrowed a reference from Theodore Shay's book, *The Legacy of the Lokmanya* (1956). Shay is an outsider and a foreign thinker, but he is allowed to enter into Golwalkar's discourse because the reference is useful for his argument:

Theodore Shay in his *The Legacy of the Lokmanya* says, 'Strangely absent from the Preamble is reference to concepts like *Swaraj*, *Dharmarajya* and the integration of the purpose of the state with the purpose of life. In other words, there is no reflection of Indian precepts or political philosophy in the Indian Constitution.'

Golwalkar criticizes the constitutional experts for importing concepts like fundamental rights from the American Constitution and the Preamble from the French Revolution. It is absurd! I've said it before, the Sangh is involved in the politics of religious faith. If you read between the lines, you will notice that the Sangh loves Hindu politics more than the Hindu religion.

It is claimed that compared to the earlier chiefs of the Sangh, its current chief, Deoras, is more liberal and a person with broad perspectives. Some of his ideas were conveyed in a speech on 'Social Equality and Hindu Organization', delivered on May 8, 1974, at the annual Vasant Vyakhyanmala (Vasant Lecture Series) organized in Pune city. I personally feel that Deoras's speech was a diplomatic tactic, so I do not feel that I must take notice of it. Ram Bapat has written extensively about it in the Marathi periodical, *Manus* (March 12 to 25, 1975).

The speech is either a complete deviation from the path presented by Golwalkar or it attempts to create an illusion while escalating his ideas. Therefore, I feel that the ideas presented in the speech are essentially the Sangh's. So it is not true that the Sangh is changing. If Deoras is arguing that the role of the Sangh has completely changed, does it imply that the ideology put forth by its previous chiefs was wrong? Deoras must articulate the change loudly and openly. At a pragmatic level, there is always some space for the old to be replaced by the new. But the various interviews of Deoras that I have come across in the post-Emergency period indicate no signs that the RSS has undergone any fundamental change. We must consider the pre-Emergency period, when he delivered a talk on the ideological role of the Sangh (in May '74). It had a different tone because of the prevailing politics, and Deoras did not wish to take a risk. His interviews now expose the same tactic of the Sangh.

Instead of discussing the changes in Deoras's attitudes, it would be apt to talk about his difficulties. The foremost trouble for Deoras is the impact of Golwalkar's personality. According to Golwalkar, those who opposed the government's policies and the communists because they are favourable towards Muslims, are not the real *swayamsevaks*. The real *swayamsevaks* are a select few of the Sangh's members, who are well-organized and who are equally the Sangh's aggressive core. It is possible that Deoras may succeed in introducing a new policy in the Sangh, but he may not succeed in transforming the young people who are under Golwalkar's influence.

The second difficulty that Deoras has encountered is the method by which Golwalkar trained the young campaigners. Golwalkar taught them to oppose socialism and democracy, and to embrace Chaturvarnya philosophy. He borrowed a well-known method about which he talks extensively in his book:

> . . . It is useless to expect that mere copying of the political and other institutions of other countries will solve our problems and bring about all-round national rejuvenation. Our malady is far deeper and requires a far more radical cure. It is to root out the basic malady that the Sangh has evolved the method of day-to-day training, the day-to-day inculcation of qualities such as the spirit of sacrifice, discipline and national devotion that go to build a resurgent and unified national life. . . . Therefore, we say let us come together in Shakha, daily and regularly. It is common experience that if a particular idea is repeated at a fixed hour regularly it goes deep into our being and becomes an inseparable part of our character. Hence the untiring stress on regularity and punctuality in the Sangh.

To illustrate his view and strengthen his argument, he narrates a story. The story is worth quoting here:

A rich man used to go to his beautiful garden in the afternoon to sit in its cool shade. One day a peacock came and sat on a tree spreading its charming feathers. The owner thought, 'How nice it would be if it comes daily at this hour!' He prepared some eatables mixed with a trace of opium and threw them before the peacock. The peacock ate them and felt elated. Next day also, the peacock came remembering that sensation of happiness and the man fed it with another dose of opium. Ultimately, the bird was so habituated that it used to come regularly at that hour even without that opium.

Golwalkar's story reveals how the Sangh uses religion and cultural egotism like a drug to oppose socialism and democracy. The story is an obvious illustration of justifying social exploitation. It emphasizes the continuation of socio-economic subjugation in society. The exploited should not resist the exploitation and so the objective should be to feed them opium every day, to lull them into a state of ignorance and subjugation. Karl Marx defined religion in similar terms.

The young peacocks of the Sangh are given ideas through the speeches of the Sangh's chiefs so that they are lulled. But are they lulled today? How can today's *sarsanghchalak* attract new *swayamsevaks* to the Sangh and shake up the old? What means can he employ to refresh them and invigorate their minds? There is a saying: the new is revived only by old medicines. This is true of the Sangh too—in the sense that there is no hope that the Sangh might change! The Sangh's growth has become increasingly complex in the last fifty years. If the new chief introduces changes in the Sangh by believing that it must change, his efforts are welcomed. However, it is quite likely that the new policies won't create a change and the chief will be left all alone.

It is impossible to imagine that the RSS will change, because it is neither a political nor a religious organization. If it were an organization meant for religion, then a religious person's mind can be influenced by explaining religion properly. Similarly, fundamental changes are possible in political organizations too. But the religious and political character of the Sangh is only an appearance—its internal philosophy is rooted in exploitation and violence. This is why the RSS chose to become a political pressure group and not a political party or a religious group—because it has no allegiance to a political ideology. The Sangh can freely refuse to accept the Flag, the Constitution, democracy and socialism because it is a pressure group. At the same time, it can take the support of ancient history and claim that everything old is in the interest of India, to further its goals. But since it cannot openly promote Chaturvarnya and class exploitation, it has to engage with politics. This is its biggest obstacle. The Sangh, which is fundamentally against democracy, does not participate in electoral politics and prefers to remain a political pressure group. It puts up a façade of being a cultural organization to avoid electoral politics. Hence, it is appropriate to regard the Sangh's views as a tendency rather than an ideology. A tendency cannot change because it is the product of vested interests. The vested interests have to be struck down to dismantle this tendency.

There is now talk of admitting Muslims into the Sangh. Deoras had shown interest in the issue, but it is a diplomatic strategy of the Sangh. Admission of non-Hindus into the Hindu organization is the demand of the day. In 1945, when a call arose to allow non-Hindus in the Hindu Mahasabha, Savarkar opposed the demand vehemently, offering an ideological explanation. He said, every political issue in India is religious and every religious issue is political. Savarkar dictated the formula to those who have played politics with the support of religion.

There are differences between the political strategies of the RSS and the Hindu Mahasabha. However, there are not many differences in their content and spirit. So, I do not expect the RSS to admit Muslims. The Savarkar principle is as applicable to the Sangh as it is to the fundamentalist Muslim organizations. It helps them play the politics of religion. Admitting non-Hindus into the Sangh would mean that the Sangh would collapse because its central principle would be affected. Those involved in Islamic politics would encounter the same, on the other hand. It seems to me that there is little possibility of any big undertaking from either side. Meanwhile, the socialist and democratic forces are hoping for the impossible to happen, and waiting with open arms to embrace them when it does—naïvely wishing that these organizations will allow democratic tendencies to sprout in them.

The political leadership of the RSS and Muslim communal forces cannot be improved through discussions. They are cautious and careful in determining the policies of their groups. 'You need to make organized efforts to destroy communal politics. Convincing, persuading or counselling are of no use in such contexts'—this piece of advice from Prof. Kurundkar is indeed apt and appropriate.

RAOSAHEB KASBE (b. 1944) is an eminent political scientist and scholar on Ambedkar and Dalit movements in India. Dr. Kasbe was Chair Professor at the Dr. Babasaheb Ambedkar Studies Centre, Savitribai Phule Pune University, from 2007 to 2014. From 1973 to 2004, he was a professor of Political Science at Sangamner College, Sangamner, Ahmednagar. He was nominated President, Maharashtra Sahitya Parishad, in 2016—the first Dalit person in that position in the institution's 113-year history.

His first book, *Zot* ('Searchlight'), was first published in 1978. His other notable works include *Dr Ambedkar ani Bharatiya Rajyaghatna* ('Dr. Ambedkar and Indian State Formation', 1978), *Ambedkar ani Marx* ('Ambedkar and Marx', 1985), *Hindu Muslim Prashna ani Savarkarancha Hindu Rashtravad* ('The Hindu Muslim Question and Savarkar's Hindu Nationalism', 1994), *Manav ani Dharma Chintan* ('Man and Religious Discourse', 1996), *Dharma Granth ani Manavi Jeevanpravah* ('Religious Scriptures and the Flow of Human Life', 2008) and *Bhakti ani Dhamma* ('Bhakti and Dhamma', 2015).

Dr. Kasbe has received many awards and honours, notably the Maharashtra and Marathwada Sahitya Parishad Puraskar, and Maharashtra Foundation's Jeevan Gaurav Puraskar.
He lives in Nasik, Maharashtra.

DEEPAK BORGAVE holds a Ph.D. in Translation Studies and an M.Phil. in Modern British Poetry. He has translated over a dozen books. His translation of *Gujarat Files* by Rana Ayyub into Marathi was published in 2018. He is a bilingual poet and critic. He lives in Pune.

SHAMSUL ISLAM is a left activist, author, and theatreperson based in Delhi. His notable books include *Know the RSS* (2000), *Golwalkar's We, or Our Nationhood Defined* (2006), and *Muslims Against Partition* (2015).

VINUTHA MALLYA is an editor and journalist based in Pune.

CPSIA information can be obtained
at www.ICGtesting.com
Printed in the USA
LVHW012337250720
661537LV00022B/2857

9 788194 077824